Is That an Unlucky Leprechaun in Your Lunch?

Is That an Unlucky Leprechaun in Your Lunch?

by Todd Strasser

SCHOLASTIC INC.

New York Toronto London Auckland Sydney
Mexico City New Delhi Hong Kong Buenos Aires

ISBN-13: 978-0-545-11034-1
ISBN-10: 0-545-11034-3

12 11 10 9 8 7 6 5 4 3 2 1   9 10 11 12 13 14/0

Printed in the U.S.A.
First printing, March 2009

Now that baseball has officially passed cricket, soccer, darts, rugby, and the caber toss[1] to become the most popular sport in all of Great Britain, this book is dedicated to two of Her Majesty's most promising future home run hitters, Conrad and Enzo Scrivener.

T.S.

---

[1] Seeing who can throw a telephone pole the farthest. No joke. This is a serious sport over there. Those Brits really are crazy!

AUTHOR'S NOTE AND WARNING

Stop! Who told you to read this book? Can't you find anything better to do? What's on TV? How about Guitar Hero? Come on, there has to be something better than this.

Seriously. It's not like you're going to get Accelerated Reader credits for reading this book. You only get Accelerated Reader credits for reading good books that expand your horizons. Reading this book will probably shrink your horizons. It's just one big waste of time. The author ought to know. He wrote it.

Besides, there are now 6,307 books in the Tardy Boys series and you're only on Book Five. You can't possibly read them all, so what's the point of even starting? The author suggests that you quit while you're ahead. Or, quit while you're abehind. Either way, DON'T READ THIS BOOK!

You're still there? What's wrong with you? You were told to stop reading. You better listen because if you continue you're going to learn about the author's IMPORTANT NEW EMERGENCY POLICY REGARDING UNDERWEAR AND UNDERPANTS.

Don't know when to quit, do you? Okay, you asked for it. Don't say we didn't warn you.

IMPORTANT NEW EMERGENCY POLICY REGARDING UNDERWEAR AND UNDERPANTS

As you may know from reading the previous Tardy Boys books, the author guarantees that the words UNDERWEAR and UNDERPANTS will not appear in these pages.

However, it has been pointed out by many readers that just because these WORDS do not appear does not mean that there are no UNDERWEAR or UNDERPANTS in these books. Readers have been quick to note that UNDERPANTS and UNDERWEAR could be hiding in drawers or hampers, on clotheslines, under couches, and in the darkest recesses of closets.

This is why the author has decided to institute an IMPORTANT NEW EMERGENCY POLICY REGARDING UNDERWEAR AND UNDERPANTS: If you, the reader, detect the presence of UNDERWEAR or UNDERPANTS take the following steps immediately:

1) the fox-trot
2) the hokey pokey
3) the Teletubby boogie-woogie

Most important, do not touch the UNDERWEAR or UNDERPANTS, as this could result in loss of appetite, headache, muscle pain, and an extreme case of the heebie-jeebies.

A FRESHLY WASHED TOE NOTE GUARANTEE

Authors of big, thick, hard-to-read books sometimes put footnotes at the bottoms of pages. Footnotes give readers extra information about whatever the author is writing. Footnotes get their name because they appear at the bottom, or foot, of the page.

Like feet, footnotes tend to be big and

smelly. For that reason, the author promises to use only freshly washed toe notes in this book. Freshly washed toe notes are much smaller than footnotes, and a lot less smellier.

THE MYSTERIOUS
CASE OF
THE TIC
OF THE FACE

It was February, a month known for the following national holidays: Groundhog Day, Laugh and Get Rich Day, Valentine's Day, Northern Hemisphere Hoodie-Hoo Day,[2] Introduce a Girl to

---

[2] At noon on Hoodie-Hoo Day, people go outside and yell "Hoodie-Hoo!" to scare away the winter and welcome the spring.

Engineering Day, and National Tooth
Fairy Day.

Nowhere in the month of February is
there a day called TJ Tardy Runs into the
Kitchen Screaming Day. But that did not
stop TJ from celebrating it.

"Ahhhhhhhhhhhhhhhh!" TJ ran into
the kitchen, screaming. He was also
scraping his face with his fingernails.

Wade Tardy looked up from the kitchen
table where he was having a bowl of
Chocolate Lucky Charms for breakfast.
"What are you doing, TJ?" he asked.

TJ did not answer. Instead he ran
around the kitchen table screaming,
"Ahhhhhhhhhhhhhhhh!"

The sound of TJ's screams brought
Wade's much handsomer twin brother,
Leyton, into the kitchen.

"Why is TJ screaming?" Leyton asked.

Wade scratched his bare head, which he had shaved at the end of Book Four in this widely read and easy-to-enjoy series. "I don't know."

"Ahhhhhhhhhhhhhhhh!" Still screaming, TJ ran out of the kitchen. *Smash! Bang! Crunk!* Loud crashing sounds came from the living room as TJ collided with various pieces of furniture.

Leyton ran his fingers through his beautiful, manageable, flowing, blond locks, which he had been born with long before this easily read and widely enjoyed series began. "Why is TJ colliding with various pieces of furniture?" he asked.

"As long as he keeps clawing at his face, he probably can't see where he's going," Wade said. "I sure hope he doesn't destroy any family heirlooms."

"That wouldn't bother me," said Leyton. "I don't plan on putting my hair in a loom anytime soon."

TJ ran back into the kitchen. He climbed onto the kitchen table and jumped up and down. "Ahhhhhhhhhhhhhhhh!" he screamed, and raked at his face.

On the kitchen table, the soggy Chocolate Lucky Charms in Wade's bowl rippled like a tar pit[3] in an earthquake. Wade looked into the bowl and wondered why he would eat anything that resembled a tar pit.

Leyton wondered why anyone would put their hair in a hair loom.

The author wondered when either Tardy boy would get around to asking TJ

---

[3] A tar pit is created when subterranean bitumen (asphalt) leaks to the surface.

why he was jumping up and down on the kitchen table, screaming and clawing at his face.

"Why are you jumping up and down on the kitchen table, screaming and clawing at your face, TJ?" asked Wade.

"Because my teacher told me I have a facial tic!" TJ screamed.[4] "And I want to get it off!"

Then he leaped down from the table and ran out of the room.

---

[4] The editor of this thoroughly researched and carefully written series has pointed out that this scene takes place in the morning. If TJ's teacher told him about the facial tic yesterday, why did TJ wait until this morning to freak out? The answer is: Because the author said so.

A LITTLE POINTY-EARED MAN

The doorbell rang.

"It's Daisy," said Wade. "Go let her in."

"Why don't *you* go let her in?" asked Leyton, who hated when his brother bossed him around.

"Whoever stays in the kitchen will have to finish eating these soggy Chocolate Lucky Charms even though they look like a tar pit," said Wade.

Leyton had never seen a tar pit. He wondered if it looked like a peach pit, an olive pit, or a double coconut palm pit, which could weigh up to sixty pounds. And while he didn't like it when his brother bossed him around, he understood that few things in the world were grosser than a bowl of soggy Chocolate Lucky Charms.[5]

"Okay," Leyton said. "I'll go let Daisy in, but only because I'd rather walk on a carpet than eat a tar pit." He went to the front door. Outside, it was a hazy gray eighty-five-degree February morning.

---

[5] The editor of this book thinks this would be a good place to mention that soggy Chocolate Lucky Charms are even grosser than Nutricat Deluxe with mustard and soy sauce. But the author disagrees. Tough noogies, Mr. Editor!

Thanks to global warming, the temperature was expected to reach ninety-seven degrees by mid-afternoon. Thanks to global pollution, the gray sky was awash with photochemical smog.

Standing on the walk outside the front door was the Tardy Boys' close friend Daisy Peduncle. Daisy's parents were hippies and Daisy was their peace-and-love child. Daisy's long brown hair was braided and she wore rose-colored granny glasses. Today she was barefoot and wore a purple tie-dyed sundress.

With Daisy was a girl with smooth dark skin and large dark eyes. She was wearing a pink scarf on her head and a long green dress with long sleeves and a high neck.

"Hi, Leyton," said Daisy. "This is my friend Madeeha Makaarim Muhammad. But she doesn't mind if you call her 3-M."

"Hi, 3-M," said Leyton.

"Ahhhhhhhhhhhhhhhhh!" Still clawing at his face, TJ dashed past them and out into the front yard, where he ran around the broken bicycles, smashed skateboards, bent Razor scooters, partly burned sofas, and cracked toilets with trees growing out of them. Then he went back inside.

"Why was TJ running around screaming and scratching at his face?" asked Daisy.

"His teacher told him he has a facial tic and he can't get it off," Leyton said. "You guys want to come in? Wade hasn't finished eating his tar pit yet."

Daisy and 3-M followed Leyton down the carpeted hallway and into the kitchen, where Wade was sitting next to a small man with a brown beard and pointy ears. The man was wearing a green hat and clothes and had a long clay pipe clenched between his teeth. Tied to his belt were two small pouches.

"This is Brendan," said Wade.

"Yo, Brendan, 'sup?" asked Leyton.

The little man shrugged and didn't answer. He stared sadly at the floor.

"Brendan's kind of bummed," said Wade.

"Where'd he come from?" Daisy asked.

"I don't know," said Wade. "I was sitting here eating soggy Chocolate Lucky Charms and all of a sudden there he was."

"Ahhhhhhhhhhhhhhhh!" TJ ran into the kitchen, grabbing at his face. He circled the kitchen table twice and then ran out.

"Wade, this is my friend Madeeha Makaarim Muhammad," said Daisy. "You can call her 3-M."

"Pleased to meet you, 3-M." Wade shook her hand. Then he checked his watch and slid his chair back. "It's time to go to school."

From upstairs came another loud crash as TJ collided with another piece of furniture.

"Don't you think you should do something about your little brother?" asked Daisy.

"I guess," said Wade.

THE
EARTH
MOVED ♥

Leyton and Wade hid at the bottom of
the stairs while Daisy called up to the
second floor: "TJ, I can help you with your
facial tic."

When TJ came downstairs, Wade and
Leyton tackled him. They held him down
and stuffed a dish towel in his mouth so
that he couldn't scream anymore. Then
they leaned close and studied his face.

"I don't see a tic," said Wade.

"Neither do I," said Leyton.

Neither Daisy nor 3-M saw a tic. Brendan, the little man dressed in green, just sighed sadly and gazed off into space. After making TJ promise not to scream anymore, Wade took the dish towel out of his little brother's mouth.

"Maybe you should go to school and ask your teacher to show you that facial tic because none of us can see it," Wade said.

TJ said he would, and everyone left the house. As they walked toward The School With No Name, Leyton looked up at the gray sky. "Didn't there used to be a hot round yellow thing up there?"

"Like a spotlight?" TJ guessed.

"Sort of," said Leyton. "But it only came out during the day."

"Oh, you mean the sun," said 3-M.

"That's it!" Leyton said. "Whatever happened to it?"

"It's still up there," said Daisy. "We just can't see it anymore."

"How come?" asked Leyton.

"I know what Al-Ian would say," said Wade. "He'd say the Shade Aliens from the Planet Curtain in the Window Treatment Galaxy are hiding it."

"Actually, we can no longer see the sun because it is permanently hidden by photochemical smog caused by all the pollution we've put in the air by driving gasoline-powered cars and using energy from coal-burning power plants," Daisy explained.

"You mean, that gray stuff up there isn't clouds?" asked TJ.

"It's clouds made of water vapor and

dangerous, poisonous chemicals," said Daisy.[6]

The Tardy Boys continued to walk to school beneath the moist, dangerous, poisonous clouds. As usual, their good friend Al-Ian Konspiracy waited for them at the corner. Al-Ian was a friendly boy and a brainiac who believed that aliens wanted to kidnap him and dissect his brain. To prevent them from doing that, he went to school each day wearing a Velostat Thought-Screen Helmet and football shoulder pads covered with aluminum foil.

"Hi, Al-Ian," Daisy said. "We were just talking about you."

"Were you wondering if I'd been kidnapped by aliens?" Al-Ian asked.

---

[6] This little toe note went to market.

"No," said Wade. "We were wondering if you would say that we can't see the sun because Shade Aliens from the Planet Curtain in the Window Treatment Galaxy are hiding it."

"Oh, be serious, Wade," Al-Ian said. "Everyone knows there's no such thing as Shade Aliens. The reason we can't see the sun is because of the Sunblock Aliens from the Planet SPF–80 in the Greasy Galaxy."

Then Al-Ian saw 3-M, and the Earth Moved ♥.[7]

---

[7] This is a metaphor for love. Poets invented metaphors for love (sometimes called terms of endearment) because their teachers were taking points off their papers for repeating the word *love* too often. To avoid confusion, the symbol ♥ will appear whenever a metaphor for love is used in this book.

DON'T PUT A MULE IN THE POOL

When the Earth Moved ♥, the Tardy
Boys, Daisy, TJ, and Brendan staggered
and nearly fell over.

"What was that?" TJ gasped.

"It felt like an earthquake," said
Daisy.

3-M looked back at Al-Ian and His Heart
Skipped a Beat ♥.

"Did you hear that?" asked Leyton.

"Sounded like a heart that skipped a beat," said Wade.

As they continued toward school, Al-Ian Only Had Eyes for 3-M ♥. But luckily, the others could see where they were going. Soon TJ said good-bye and went off toward the elementary school, where he planned to ask his teacher to find his facial tic. The Tardy Boys and their friends kept walking. Only now Leyton bit his lip and began to look around nervously.

"What's wrong?" asked Daisy.

"This is the part of the book where Barton Slugg always attacks us," said Leyton.

No sooner did those words leave Leyton's mouth than Barton Slugg, the Tardy Boys' WORST ARCHENEMY EVER, stepped out from behind a tree. Barton had buckteeth and brown hair that fell into his beady little eyes. On his face was an evil grin. On his shoulder was a huge orange-red-and-blue Super Drencher Water Bazooka. In the tank was an ominous-looking green liquid.

"Put your hands up!" Barton ordered.

The Tardy Boys and their friends fearfully raised their hands.

"Did you hear about the new rule at school?" Barton asked.

"Is the new rule at school that you're not allowed to drool?" asked Al-Ian.

"No," said Barton.

"Is the new rule at school that it's uncool to be a fool?" asked Leyton.

"No," said Barton.

"Is the new rule at school that you can't put a mule in the pool?" asked Wade.

"No," said Barton. "The new rule at

school is that anyone who's late will be permanently expelled."

"Then we better get to school," said 3-M.

"Not so fast," said Barton. "It's going to cost you money to get past me."

"But we don't have any money," said Wade.

"Then you're going to be late and that means you'll be expelled forever," said Barton.

"If we're expelled from school forever, you'll never see Daisy again," Wade said. "And you won't be able to write her any more anonymous love poems."[8]

---

[8] See *Is That a Glow-in-the-Dark Bunny in Your Pillowcase?* for more information about these remarkable and badly spelled poems.

At the thought of never seeing Daisy again, Barton wiped a tear from his eye and quoted Alfred, Lord Tennyson,[9] "It is better to have loved and lost than never to have loved at all."

Daisy's eyes softened. "Barton, you quoted a love poem! That's so sweet! But what makes you think you can stop us just because you've got a Super Drencher Water Bazooka on your shoulder?"

"Because this Super Drencher Water Bazooka isn't filled with water," Barton said with an evil smile. "It's filled with ultra-concentrated box jellyfish venom!"

---

[9] British poet and shortstop who hit the winning home run in the historic twenty-three-inning game between the Nottingham Nitwits and Liverpool Loons.

The Tardy Boys and their friends shrank back in fear. There was nothing in THE ENTIRE UNIVERSE more deadly than ultra-concentrated box jellyfish venom.

"So cough it up," Barton said.

The Tardy Boys and their friends shared puzzled looks. Then they put their hands in front of their mouths and started to cough.

"No, you fools," Barton snarled. "'Cough it up' is an idiom. It means give me some money."

"Boy, do I hate idioms," Leyton muttered.

"I already told you we don't have any money," said Wade.

Barton aimed the Super Drencher Water Bazooka at Brendan. "What about the leprechaun?"

"Hush!" Daisy pressed her finger to her lips. "Don't call him that. The politically correct term is little pointy-eared mythological being of Irish descent."

Barton rolled his eyes impatiently. "Whatever!"

Meanwhile, the Tardy Boys and their friends huddled.

"What are we going to do?" whispered Al-Ian.

"Maybe we should try an end run," whispered Wade.

"What's that?" asked 3-M.

"I don't know," said Wade. "But it's what people say when they're in a situation like this. When I count to three, everyone run."

QUEEN
FOR
A DAY

The Tardy Boys and their friends faced Barton.

"One," counted Wade. "Two."

"Don't tell me you're going to try an end run," said Barton.

"How'd you know?" asked Al-Ian.

"Because it's the oldest trick in the book," Barton said. "Can't you think of something new?"

Brendan reached into one of the small pouches at his waist and took out a gold coin.

Barton snatched it out of the little man's hand. "Real gold!" he cried. "I'm rich! I can't believe you fell for it! This isn't ultra-concentrated box jellyfish venom! It's green sports drink!"

Barton ran away laughing. Afraid of getting expelled, the Tardy Boys and their friends hurried toward school.

"Dude, thanks for giving Barton that gold coin," Wade said to Brendan.

Brendan nodded sadly. When the Tardy Boys and their friends got to The School With No Name, Assistant Principal Snout was standing at the entrance wearing a white breathing mask, bright yellow foam earplugs, and light-blue latex gloves. Ulna Mandible was screaming at him while her daughter, Fibby, stood behind her. Fibby had streaked blonde hair and a freckled nose.

"If you don't have a St. Patrick's Day parade, I'll sue!" Ulna yelled.

"Why do you want us to have a parade?" asked Assistant Principal Snout.

"Because my daughter, Fibby, wants to be queen of the parade!" bellowed Ulna.[10] *"And she can't be queen of the parade if there is no parade!"*

Assistant Principal Snout looked at his wristwatch. "The bell just rang. I'm sure you don't want your daughter to be

---

[10] In the first four books of this scintillating series, Ulna only knew five ways to speak: shouting, yelling, screaming, screeching, and shrieking. But recently she's begun experimenting with hollering and bellowing.

expelled for being late. I promise I'll look into having a St. Patrick's Day parade."

"*You better!*" Ulna Mandible hollered, and then got into her bright red Hummer and roared away.

Fibby went into school. Assistant Principal Snout sighed sadly and turned to the Tardy Boys and their friends. "What am I going to do about her?"

"You could stop letting her boss you around," said Daisy.

Assistant Principal Snout turned pale. "Are you crazy? She'd have me fired. And then I'd have to go out into the real world where people actually have to be good at something. The only thing I'm good at is punishing kids. That reminds me. You're all late. Go to my office and wait there for me to expel you."

Just then Barton came down the

sidewalk. Wade pointed at him. "Shouldn't Barton be expelled, too?"

Assistant Principal Snout turned to Barton. "Why are you late?"

Barton pointed at Brendan. "Because that leprechaun gave me a gold coin that turned to dust[11] and I had to go back home and wash all the dust off my hands."

"I certainly appreciate that," said Assistant Principal Snout. "We don't want children coming to school with dusty hands. You may go in."

Barton pointed a freshly washed finger at Brendan. "You're going to be so sorry," he snarled, and went into school.

---

[11] This is what usually happens when a little pointy-eared mythological being of Irish descent gives you a gold coin.

NATIONAL TOOTH FAIRY DAY

The Tardy Boys and their friends went into school. Hanging across the entrance was a brand-new banner:

WELCOME TO THE SCHOOL WITH NO NAME
"A NATIONAL BLUE RIBBON GERMFREE SCHOOL"

They went down the hall to the office. Before they could enter, they had to

brush and floss their teeth, remove
their shoes, and wash their hands. While
he washed his hands, Leyton looked at a
new sign hanging over the sink.

WASH HANDS WITH LIQUID SOAP UNDER WARM
RUNNING WATER FOR AT LEAST FIVE MINUTES.

PAY SPECIAL ATTENTION TO GERMS THAT MAY BE
TRAPPED UNDER NAILS AND IN CREVICES.

DRY HANDS WITH PAPER TOWELS. USE A PAPER
TOWEL TO TURN OFF THE FAUCET.

Leyton lifted his hands and stared at his
fingers.[12]

"What are you doing?" asked Daisy.

"Paying special attention to germs that
may be trapped under nails and in
crevices," Leyton said.

---

[12] This little toe note stayed home.

"You can't *see* them, silly," said Daisy. "They're microscopic."

"But the sign says I should pay special attention to them," Leyton said.

"That's misleading," said Wade.

"I thought Miss Leading was the girls' gym teacher," said Leyton.

"That's a different Miss Leading," said Daisy. "Germs are way too small to see. In your mouth alone there are more than three hundred different types of bacteria, but you can't see any of them."

"Maybe they're hiding," said Leyton.

"Would you finish washing already?" Wade said impatiently. "We're all waiting for you."

Leyton hated it when his brother got impatient. "Go ahead," he said. "I'll be there in slightly more than five minutes."

The others went into the office. Meanwhile, Leyton washed and dried his hands. But it wasn't easy to follow the rest of the sign's instructions.

After a while, Wade came back out to see what was taking Leyton so long. He found his brother surrounded by a mound of torn-and-crumpled paper towels. The faucet was still running.

"What are you doing?" Wade asked.

"Trying to turn off the faucet with a paper towel," Leyton said. "But the towels keep tearing."

Wade put a paper towel over the faucet handle and turned it off. Then he gave his brother *The Look*.

Leyton hated *The Look*. It meant that Wade still thought his skull was so empty that monkeys could swing from the branches of the trees inside.

"Don't give me that look!" Leyton yelled angrily. "You know that ever since Book Three in this series there have been billions of brand-new teensy-weensy, itsy-bitsy brain cells growing inside my skull.[13] And thanks to them I've had some really good ideas."

"Not in this book, you haven't," said Wade.

"Give me time," said Leyton. "We're only on page thirty-nine."

"What if your brain cells took the day off?" asked Wade.

Leyton felt a sudden chill. "What day is it?"

"February twenty-eighth," said his brother. "National Tooth Fairy Day. And

---

[13] See *Is That a Glow-in-the-Dark Bunny in Your Pillowcase?* for more information about these remarkably teensy-weensy brain cells.

brain cells don't have teeth. So I bet they hitched rides to the beach."

The news stunned Leyton. No wonder he hadn't had an idea that day! It was so unfair! He'd had to wait two whole books in this series until the author gave him brain cells, and now the author had taken them away again! It wasn't just unfair, it was cruel and inhuman!

Leyton made a fist and muttered, "Darn you, Mr. Author!" Then he hung his head sadly. His gorgeous, manageable, flowing, blond locks fell into his eyes as he trudged into Assistant Principal Snout's office. It was just his luck to have an author who let his brain cells go to the beach on National Tooth Fairy Day.

AL-IAN'S SUN, MOON, AND STARS ♥

Inside the office a thick pane of bulletproof glass stretched from the floor to the ceiling, separating Assistant Principal Snout's desk from some chairs lined up against the opposite wall. The Tardy Boys and their friends sat in the chairs. After a moment, a bookcase on the other side of the bulletproof glass swung open and the assistant principal stepped through the secret doorway. He sat down at his desk and removed his bright yellow earplugs. Now that he was safe in his office, he did not have to fear THE SHRIEK OF ULNA MANDIBLE. He also took off his breathing mask. Thanks to his hypoallergenic air purifier, he did not have to worry about breathing the same air that students breathed. He also took off his blue latex gloves. Now that he was on the other side of the bulletproof glass, he did not have to worry about being touched by germ-ridden young people.

Assistant Principal Snout pressed a button on his desk and spoke through a microphone, "Are you ready to be expelled?"

"Isn't that a really harsh punishment just for being late?" asked Daisy.

"Harsh?" repeated the assistant principal. "You want to know what's harsh? Thanks to Ulna Mandible, I have to plan an entire St. Patrick's Day parade! That's harsh! Why should I have to do it? Why can't someone else do it? Someone who isn't as busy as I am punishing students and stopping the spread of germs." He pointed at Daisy, Leyton, and Wade. "In fact, I'm so busy I don't have time to expel anyone. You three go to your classrooms." Then he pointed at Brendan and 3-M. "You two go to the ESL class."

"No!" cried Al-Ian. "You can't send her to the ESL class!"

"Why not?" asked the assistant principal.

Al-Ian didn't know how to answer. How could he explain that to be away from The Apple of His Eye ♥ for even a moment would feel like The Sun Had Stopped Shining ♥, like The Birds Had Lost Their Song ♥, like The World Was Coming to an End ♥?

But then Al-Ian realized THE TERRIBLE TRUTH! Thanks to photochemical smog, the sun *had* stopped shining. And thanks to avian tonsillitis,[14] the birds *had* stopped singing. And, thanks to all the dumb stuff humans were doing to the earth, the world might very well *be* coming to an end!

And that meant that Assistant Principal Snout probably *could* send His Sun, Moon, and Stars ♥ to the ESL class.

The Tardy Boys and their friends went back out into the hall.

---

[14] Birds have something called cecal tonsils, but the author isn't sure where they are located or what birds need them for.

"I can't believe you and Brendan have to go to the ESL class," Daisy said to 3-M. "Your English is just as good as everyone else's. And we don't know how Brendan's English is because he's too depressed to speak."

"It's okay," 3-M replied. "Your assistant principal thinks I need to be in the ESL class because I look different. But when the ESL teacher hears how well I speak English, she will recommend that I switch to the regular classes."

Leyton turned to Brendan and said, "Dude, how come you're so bummed?"

The little pointy-eared mythological being of Irish descent just shrugged.

"This is a wild guess," said Al-Ian, "but I'd bet it has something to do with his pot of gold."

Brendan jerked his head up with a

surprised look, then nodded sadly and stared at the floor.

"It makes sense," agreed Wade. "I mean, why else would he be hanging around here? He must be looking for his gold."

Again, Brendan nodded sadly.

Just then Fibby and Barton Slugg came running around the corner. "There he is!" Barton pointed at Brendan. "He's the one who gave me that phony gold coin!"

EVERYONE LOVES MONEY

Fibby and Barton rushed toward them. At the same time, the Tardy Boys and their friends looked around, but Brendan was gone.[15]

"Where'd he go?" Leyton asked.

"It's like he vanished," said Daisy.

---

[15] Little pointy-eared mythological beings of Irish descent are very fast and difficult to catch.

Barton started looking everywhere — in classrooms and lockers, around corners and in closets. "I'm going to find that leprechaun and make him give me a new gold coin," he grumbled. "And the next one better be real."

"Dude," Leyton said with a chuckle. "Why bother looking for just one gold coin when there's probably a *whole pot* of gold around here somewhere?"

Wade kicked his brother in the shin. "You numbskull!"

"Ow!" Leyton grabbed his leg and jumped around on one foot. Meanwhile, Barton's and Fibby's eyes lit up.

"A whole pot of gold!!!!" Fibby gasped.

"I'm going to find it!" Barton ran off down the hall.

"Not if I find it first!" Fibby ran in another direction.

Wade turned to Leyton, who was rubbing his sore shin. "Why'd you tell them about the pot of gold? If Barton and Fibby find it before Brendan does they'll never give it back. And then we'll be stuck with that depressed little pointy-eared mythological being of Irish descent for the rest of our lives!"

"It's not my fault," Leyton said with a sniff. "How was I supposed to know the heartless author of this book was going to tell my brain cells to take off National Tooth Fairy Day and go to the beach? If you have to blame someone, blame him!"

It was time to go to class. Al-Ian gave The Fairest Girl in All the Land ♥ a sad wave, and she went off toward the ESL classroom. The Tardy Boys and their friends went to Ms. Fitt's class. When they got there, everyone was watching a video on the large, flat-screen HDTV that had been donated to the school by the National Association of Television Manufacturers. The video was titled "Why You and Everyone You Know Should Use Lots and Lots of Thunderwear®™ Deluxe Crystal-Clear Germ-Massacring Hand Sanitizer."

Daisy raised her hand. "We watched this video yesterday. Why are we watching it again?"

Ms. Fitt looked up from her computer, where she was busy answering e-mails. She had red hair that hung past her shoulders in ringlets. "Assistant Principal Snout says every time we watch this video, the United Thunderwear®™ Corporation pays him twenty-five dollars. So he wants us to watch it at least once a day."

Daisy angrily balled her hands into fists.

"Why does everything have to be about money?"

"Good question," said Ms. Fitt. "Let me see if there's a video here that has the answer." She began to look through the rows of DVDs on the shelves that used to hold books before most of the books were thrown out to make room for the DVDs.

"Wait," said Daisy. "Instead of watching another video, can't we talk about it?"

Ms. Fitt straightened up and looked surprised. "You mean, have a classroom discussion?"

"Yes," said Daisy.

Ms. Fitt turned to the other students. "Daisy has suggested that we participate in something called a dialogue."

A kid named Andy Kent raised his hand. "How does it work?"

"First we agree on the topic to be discussed," Daisy said. "In this case that would be the American obsession with money. Then we raise our hands and express our opinions."

"You mean, like on *Deal or No Deal* when people in the audience yell out whether they think the person should take the deal or not take the deal?" asked a boy named Josh Hopka.

"Something like that," said Daisy. "Only it's important to listen and think about what the other people are saying."

Just then, the classroom door opened and Fibby and Barton came in. Fibby frowned. "Why aren't we watching TV?"

"We've decided to have a dialogue about why it seems like money is the only thing anyone cares about," said Ms. Fitt.

"What's to discuss?" asked Fibby.

"That's the way it's always been. The only time it wasn't that way was in the 1960s, when hippies tried to tell everyone that peace and love were more important than money."

"Fibby's right," said Barton. "Look at what happened during the California Gold Rush. People left their families and friends and jobs and rushed to California to look for gold. They wouldn't have done that if they didn't love money."

"That's not how you measure love," argued Daisy.

"Al-Ian," said Ms. Fitt. "If you loved something, would you leave your family and friends and job for it?"

Al-Ian thought of his Sweet Darling Only One ♥. Surely he would leave his family and friends and job for her. Especially since he had no job. "Yes," he said.

Fibby grinned meanly at Daisy. "See? Even your own friend disagrees with you."

"There's one thing I don't understand," said Barton. "Just because you find something doesn't mean it's yours, does it? If I find someone's cell phone, it still belongs to the person who owns it. So why, if someone finds gold, can they say it's theirs?"

"Thanks to the General Mining Act of 1872,[16] gold belongs to whomever finds it first," said Ms. Fitt.

Barton smiled broadly. "Great! So, if I find that pot of gold, it's going to be all mine!"

---

[16] The General Mining Act of 1872 allowed any citizen of the United States to stake a claim to valuable minerals like gold and silver. This should not be confused with the General Miming Act of 1972, which allowed people to act out stories through body motions without the use of speech.

THE
JUMBO
ATOMIC
OMNITRON

At the end of the day the Tardy Boys and their friends walked toward the school lobby. Each of them had different thoughts. To learn what those thoughts were, you could have drilled a tiny orifice into each of their skulls and peeked inside. But, as we already know from Book Three of this phenomenal and phantasmagorical[17] series, the results of drilling holes into students' skulls are often messy, and therefore frowned upon by Assistant Principal Snout.

Hence, the author has decided to introduce a brand-new literary innovation called the Jumbo Atomic Omnitron. Using this amazing device, you, the reader, can now look into the minds of characters and see what they are thinking:

1) Wade is worried that if Barton Slugg finds Brendan's pot of gold, he will never give it back.
2) The author is wondering who told Leyton's brain cells to take off National Tooth Fairy Day, because it wasn't him. He also wonders if this has

---

[17] Like fenomenal and fantasy, only with *ph* instead of *f*.

anything to do with the three letters he has recently received in which students have written to the Arthur.

3) Daisy is worried that if all anyone cares about is money, then all the people without money will feel like no one cares about them.

4) Leyton is worried that the author might be so mean and cruel that he will extend his brain cells' vacation to the following day, National Pig Day.

5) The Jumbo Atomic Omnitron can't see through Velostat Thought-Screen Helmets. However, it is safe to guess that Al-Ian is missing His Sweet Darling One ♥.

In the school lobby, they met 3-M and Brendan. Al-Ian glanced at The One for Whom His Heart Sang ♥ and felt himself tremble with nervous excitement. "How was ESL class?" he asked.

"Boring," said 3-M. "I told the teacher that my English is already very good. She said she would watch how I progress and would let me know when I was ready for the regular classes."

"Wait a minute," said Wade. "If you spoke to her, she must have heard how good your English is."

"That's what I thought, too," said 3-M. "But she said that just because I speak English well doesn't mean it's not my second language. At The School With No Name you have to stay in ESL until English becomes your first language."

"What happens if you know two languages equally well?" asked Daisy.

"Then you go to the English as Tied for First Language class," said 3-M.

"And what if you knew three languages equally well?" asked Al-Ian.

"Then you'd go to English in a Three-Way Tie for First Language," said 3-M.

The Tardy Boys and their friends started toward home. Suddenly they heard the high-pitched sound of a small motor. Barton Slugg was coming toward them on a shiny new BladeX motorized scooter. He stopped near them and quoted Aristotle,[18] "Love is a single soul inhabiting two bodies."

"Barton, you quoted love poetry again!" Daisy gushed.

---

[18] Greek philosopher and pitcher who threw a no-hitter for the Athens Angels in the seventh game of the 367 B.C. World Series against the Sparta Nosox.

"And I've got a brand-new motorized scooter and those guys don't," Barton said, pointing at the Tardy Boys.

"That scooter looks expensive," said Wade. "How did you get the money to pay for it?"

"I guess you could say that I 'lucked' into it." Barton revved up his scooter and rode away.

No sooner did Barton leave than Ulna and Fibby Mandible drove up in their big red Hummer. On both sides of the Hummer were banners saying:

CELEBRATE THE FEAST OF THE MILLIONAIRE NUN

(AND NOT THAT OTHER HOLIDAY)

ON MARCH 17

Fibby got out with a ticket book. "Ready to buy tickets for the brand-new national holiday on March seventeenth?"

NATIONAL WIPE OUT METAPHORS AND IDIOMS MONTH

"Isn't March seventeenth St. Patrick's Day?" Al-Ian asked.

"Not anymore," said Fibby. "We're replacing it with the Feast of the Millionaire Nun."

"Why?" asked Daisy.

"Because we believe in REAL saints!" bellowed Ulna. *"And no one can absolutely prove that St. Patrick was REAL."*

Wade turned to Brendan. "Is that true?"

Brendan rolled his eyes as if to say, "Who knows?" 3-M took out a small bright red handheld device.

"What's that?" asked Fibby.

"A Swiss Army BlackBerry," said 3-M. "The only device that can access the Internet, send e-mail, act as a cell phone, and open a can of baked beans."

"Mom, I want you to buy me one of those today," Fibby demanded.

In the meantime, 3-M logged on to the Internet. "There may have actually been two people who together are thought of as St. Patrick."[19]

---

[19] This is called the "Two Patricks" theory. There is also the "Nine Patricks" theory, which contends that St. Patrick was actually a team in the old Irish baseball league.

"But this morning you told Assistant Principal Snout that you wanted him to have the St. Patrick's Day parade so that Fibby could be the queen," Daisy said to Ulna.

"There are more important things than being queen of a parade," said Fibby. "And one of them is being a REAL human and not a mythological being. And that's why we're going to replace the St. Patrick's Day parade with the Feast of the Millionaire Nun."

"Was there really a millionaire nun?" asked Wade.

"Yes," said Fibby. "Her name is St. Katharine Drexel and she's an American saint. She came from a very wealthy family and used her money to build schools for poor people."

"What kind of feast will it be?" asked Leyton.

"Barbecue," said Fibby.

"Why barbecue?" asked Al-Ian.

"Because barbecue is as American as apple pie," said Fibby.

3-M checked her Swiss Army BlackBerry again. "I hate to say this, but apple pie isn't American. Recipes for apple pie go back to England in the 1300s. And barbecue isn't American, either. It is said to have come from the Caribbean."

"No one asked you," Fibby said. She turned to the Tardy Boys. "I assume you'll want five tickets."

"But there are six of us," said Leyton.

Fibby pointed at Brendan. "He can't come because he's a mythological being."

"That's mean," said Daisy. "Why would you want him to feel left out? Mythological beings have feelings just like the rest of us.

Besides, America is supposed to be the great melting pot for all people."

"They melt?" Leyton asked.

"It's a metaphor," Wade said. "People don't really melt. They just all mix together."

Leyton clenched his fists. "Know what I think is causing all the problems in the world? Metaphors and idioms. I hereby declare March National Wipe Out Metaphors and Idioms Month."

"No!" said Fibby. "I declare March National It's Great to Be a REAL Person and Not a Mythological Being Month."

"Too late," said Leyton. "I declared it National Wipe Out Metaphors and Idioms Month first."

"Wait," said Al-Ian. "Why can't it be both?"

"Because it can't," said Fibby. "A month can only be about one thing."

"That's so not true," said 3-M, and pointed at her Swiss Army BlackBerry. "For your information, March is already Adopt a Rescued Guinea Pig Month, National Frozen Food Month, National Umbrella Month, Play the Recorder Month, and Expand Girls' Horizons in Science & Engineering Month."

"Girls have horizons?" Leyton asked.

Wade gave him *The Look*.

"I hate that look!" Leyton shouted. "Just wait until tomorrow when my brain cells come back from the beach. You're going to be sorry!"

"Quiet!" Ulna hollered. "*I'm tired of all this gibberish about months and metaphors and brain cells. Just buy the tickets already.*"

"How much are they?" asked Wade.

"Ten dollars," said Fibby.

"That's expensive," said Al-Ian.

"So?" screamed Ulna.

"What if we don't have enough money?" asked Al-Ian.

"You don't need money to buy expensive things," shouted Ulna. "This is America. Nobody has enough money to buy all the things they want. That's why we have credit cards."

The Tardy Boys and their friends looked at one another. "We don't have any credit cards," said Wade.

Fibby narrowed her eyes. "Only losers don't have credit cards! Come on, Mom. We have to go find some winners with credit cards!"

Fibby and her mother jumped into the big red Hummer and roared off to find some American winners with credit cards.[20]

---

[20] This little toe note had roast beef.

SCREAMING BRAINS

The Tardy Boys and their friends continued toward their homes. But Daisy had a funny feeling. "Something isn't right."

"A left?" guessed Wade.

"A wrong?" guessed Al-Ian.

"A humpback?" guessed Leyton.

Daisy stopped. "What are you talking about?"

"A left isn't a right," said Wade.

"And a wrong isn't a right," said Al-Ian.

"And neither is a humpback or a blue or a minke," said Leyton.

"Those are whales," said 3-M.

"And none of them is a right!" realized Daisy. "Only a right whale is a right whale."

Leyton smiled proudly. "And that means I'm right!"

"Yes," said Daisy, "but that's not what I'm talking about."

Leyton grit his teeth and thought, *Wrong again! It's all YOUR fault, Mr. Author!*

Daisy turned to the others. "When I said something isn't right, I meant that this morning Ulna Mandible was totally into having a St. Patrick's Day parade. Then this afternoon she suddenly changed her mind."

"You think the Mandibles have something up their sleeves?" asked Al-Ian.

"Their arms!" Leyton gasped.

"It's an idiom," Wade told his brother. "When someone is said to have something up his sleeve, it means he is hiding something that he intends to use later."

"Like his arms!" Leyton insisted.

"Yes, but not in this case," said Daisy.

"I don't see a case," said Leyton.

"It's not a case you can see," said Daisy.

"Then what kind of case is it?" Leyton asked.

"Aaaaaaaaaaahhhhh!" Just then, TJ Tardy came running toward them screaming his brains out.

Only his brains weren't really coming out, because that is a metaphor.

When Leyton saw his little brother running toward them, he tried to think of what to do. It wasn't easy because, thanks to the mean and cruel author, his brain cells were taking off National Tooth Fairy Day. So instead of thinking, Leyton did what people without brains often do: He just reacted.

Wham! As TJ ran past, screaming his brains out, Leyton hit him with a monster cross-body block.

Pow! Leyton head-speared his little brother under the chin.

Bam! Leyton horse-collared TJ from behind and slammed him to the ground.

A second later TJ lay on his back, stunned. "Ow," he said. "Why'd you do that?"

"To stop you from running and screaming your brains out," Leyton said. "Even though that's a metaphor, you never really know when someone's brains might start coming out."

"But maybe I *felt* like running and screaming my brains out," said TJ.

"Weren't you screaming because of your facial tic?" asked Wade.

"No," said TJ. "That went away."

"How?" asked Daisy.

"It just did," said TJ. "My teacher said tics come and go. It happens to kids a lot. And it turns out that a facial tic isn't a small bloodsucking arachnid[21] that feeds on warm-blooded vertebrates.[22] That kind of tick is spelled TICK. A facial tic is a

---

[21] Arachnids include spiders, scorpions, mites, and some politicians.

[22] Vertebrates include all animals that have backbones except some politicians.

sudden, spasmodic, painless muscle contraction. It could even be a wink."

"A winky tic," said Leyton.

TJ propped himself up on his elbows and looked at the small crowd around him. "So what are you doing anyway?"

"We think Fibby Mandible and her mother are up to something and we need to figure out what it is," said Wade.

"Why?" asked TJ.

"Because if we don't, Fibby's going to change St. Patrick's Day into the Feast of the Millionaire Nun," Daisy said.

Since they were at the corner where he left them every day after school, Al-Ian gazed upon His Hunka Hunka Burnin' Love ♥, and smiled wistfully. "Until tomorrow, my darling."

The Tardy Boys, Daisy, 3-M, and Brendan continued toward home.

"Is it my imagination, or is Al-Ian acting weird?" TJ asked.

"Al-Ian is definitely acting weird," agreed Daisy.

"Do you think the Hypno Aliens[23] from the Planet Hocus in the Pocus Galaxy are using direct-hypnotic staring to gain control of his mind?" asked TJ.

"No," said Daisy.

"Are the Alien Cat Hisstorians[24] using their glowing eyes to bend him to their wills?" asked TJ.

"Not that, either," said Daisy.

---

[23] See *Is That a Dead Dog in Your Locker?* for more information about these remarkably hypnotic aliens.

[24] See *Is That a Sick Cat in Your Backpack?* for more information about these remarkably furry aliens.

"Have the giant alien hockey-stick insects[25] finally figured out how to penetrate his Velostat Thought-Screen Helmet?" asked TJ.

"No, TJ," said Daisy. "What's happened to Al-Ian happens to many growing young men who are on the verge of manhood."

"Their pants get too short?" TJ guessed.

"No," said Daisy. "They fall in love."

---

[25] See *Is That an Angry Penguin in Your Gym Bag?* for more information about these remarkably sticky aliens.

A
DULLAHAN

That night Wade spent several hours reading the dictionary in an effort to be Totally Beyond Excellent in School so that he could get a scholarship to college. Wade needed a college scholarship because his parents were being held captive on a distant planet by aliens who let them eat pizza and watch reruns of *American Idol*.

After a while, Wade went downstairs. In the kitchen he found Leyton and Brendan with a brand-new Ultrathin 18-inch, 3.4 GHz MacBook AirPro MegaSuper floating laptop.

"Dude, where did that come from?" Wade gasped. He knew that the Ultrathin 18-inch, 3.4 GHz MacBook AirPro MegaSuper was the single most expensive personal laptop computer in the entire solar system. It was so light that it actually floated.

"It's Brendan's," Leyton said. "He's IMing his mythological friends."

"Like who?" Wade asked.

"Oh, you know," said Leyton, "mermaids, pixies, other leprechauns, giants, fairies, and banshees. The usual suspects."

Wade scratched his shaved head. "Dude, I hate to tell you this, but none of those things really exist. That's why they're called mythological."

Brendan scowled at Wade. It was obvious that he disagreed.

"Then who is Brendan IMing?" Leyton asked.

"He could be IMing anyone," Wade said. "It's the Internet. Just because someone *says* he's a pixie doesn't mean he really is."

Brendan frowned and snapped his fingers.

Suddenly they heard loud clip-clopping in the hall. It sounded like a horse trotting. A second later a headless man rode a headless horse into the kitchen. The man held his head under his arm with one hand and the reins with the other. His eyes were wide and he had a huge and hideous grin. He rode around the kitchen table once and then back down the hall.

Wade felt the blood drain from his face and his scrawny body trembled. Brendan typed something on the computer.

"He says that was called a Dullahan," Leyton said. "He wants to know if you'd like to meet the sleeping giant next."

"What's the sleeping giant?" Wade asked.

Brendan typed on the computer, and Leyton read, "The sleeping giant lives under the earth and doesn't like to be disturbed. He only comes out when one of his friends needs his help. But he's really grumpy when he wakes up."

"So, if I met him, he'd be really grumpy?" Wade asked.

"And really big," said Leyton.

"I think I'll pass," said Wade.

"But we're not playing football," said Leyton.

The next morning the Tardy Boys and

their friends walked to school. Al-Ian waited for them at the corner and when he saw His One and Only ♥ dressed in a long blue dress and wearing a red head-scarf, he gave her a flower. When they got to school, Fibby and Ulna Mandible were already there. As usual, Ulna was screaming at Assistant Principal Snout.

"If you don't change the St. Patrick's Day parade into the Feast of the Millionaire Nun, I'll sue!" she shrieked.

"But yesterday you *wanted* a St. Patrick's Day parade," Assistant Principal Snout protested.

"That was yesterday! And today is today and you better do it, or else!" Ulna Mandible screamed, and then got into her bright red Hummer and roared away.

"You better listen to what she says," Fibby threatened, and went into school.

Assistant Principal Snout sighed sadly and shook his head. He turned to the Tardy Boys and their friends. "What am I going to do about those two?" he asked woefully.

For one brief moment Al-Ian tore his eyes away from The Object of His Affections ♥ and said, "You could say your identity was stolen."

Assistant Principal Snout scowled. "What do you mean?"

"If your identity gets stolen you can't be Assistant Principal Snout anymore," Al-Ian explained. "Then the next time Ulna Mandible yells at Assistant Principal Snout, she won't be yelling at you. She'll be yelling at the person who stole your identity."

Assistant Principal Snout blinked with astonishment. "That is a brilliant suggestion!"

Al-Ian smiled proudly even though being so smart made him a target for alien kidnappers from all over the universe. He adjusted his foil-covered shoulder pads and turned back to 3-M. Once again he felt as if His Heart Would Burst ♥.

Assistant Principal Snout looked at his watch and frowned. "According to the new rules, you're all expelled."

"But Al-Ian just solved all your problems with Ulna Mandible," Wade said.

Assistant Principal Snout scratched his ear thoughtfully. "You're right. It's not fair to expel you after you've solved my greatest problem. Go to my office and wait for me there."

A FOUNTAIN
OF
CLEANLINESS

The Tardy Boys and their friends
went to the office. As usual, they had to
brush and floss their teeth, remove their
shoes, and wash their hands before they
were allowed to enter. Then they waited
on their side of the bulletproof glass
for Assistant Principal Snout. After a
moment, a bookcase on the other side of
the office swung open and the assistant

principal stepped through the secret doorway.

The assistant principal swiveled his large HDTV screen around. "Please direct your attention to the screen," he said, and pressed a button on a remote. On the screen appeared a colorful painting of a large, ornate fountain in the middle of the school lobby. "This is the proposed design for our new Fountain of Cleanliness, which has been donated to the school by our good friends from the United Thunderwear®™ Corporation. As you can see, we plan to build the fountain just inside the front doors, and under the skylight."

The assistant principal clicked the remote again. This time the Fountain of Cleanliness was surrounded by students washing their hands. "Every student entering the school will be required to wash his or her hands before going to class."

Daisy raised her hand. "You showed us where the students will wash their hands, but not where they'll dry them. Won't this mean the school lobby will be littered with used paper towels?"

The assistant principal smiled broadly. "The Fountain of Cleanliness will not spout water. It will spout Thunderwear®™ Deluxe Crystal-Clear Germ-Massacring Hand Sanitizer! There'll be no need for paper towels. Just picture it. The sunlight coming down through the skylight, making the Thunderwear®™ Deluxe Crystal-Clear Germ-Massacring Hand Sanitizer sparkle as it flows over the hands of the students eager to massacre each and every one of those disgusting germs clinging to their skin.[26] Brilliant, isn't it?"

Neither the Tardy Boys nor their friends responded. The corners of the assistant principal's mouth turned down. He had expected them to break into spontaneous cheers and applause. "Why are you here?"

"Because you said we were late," answered Wade.

The assistant principal shook his head. "No, I didn't."

"Yes, you did," said Daisy. "Just a little while ago in front of the school."

"Not me," said the assistant principal. "The person who told you to come to this office was probably Assistant

_____

[26] Scientific fact: Nearly ten million bacteria live in the inside crease of the average human's elbow.

Principal Snout, but his identity has been stolen."

"Then who are you?" asked Leyton, who was still not sure if his brain cells were back.

"I am the Assistant Principal Once Known as Snout," said the person sitting at the desk. "Or the APOKS, for short."

BRATA-RATA-BRATA-RATA! Suddenly a very loud racket filled the office. The floor began to shake and vibrate.

"The earth is moving again!" Al-Ian cried.

"Earthquake!" Wade gasped.

"Subway train!" cried Leyton.

"No! It's the United Thunderwear®™ Corporation!" the APOKS shouted happily. "They've begun digging the Fountain of Cleanliness! I must go see!" He jumped up from his desk and disappeared through the secret doorway in the bookshelf.

The Tardy Boys and their friends left the office and went out into the hall. *BRATA-RATA-BRATA-RATA!* The sound was even louder and the floor shook even harder.

"I can't believe they're doing construction during the school day," Wade shouted over the roar.

"Look!" 3-M pointed down the hall where Fibby and Ulna Mandible were taping a big red-white-and-blue poster to the wall. The poster said:

CELEBRATE

THE FEAST OF THE MILLIONAIRE NUN

(AND NOT THAT OTHER HOLIDAY)

ON MARCH 17

AT THE SCHOOL WITH NO NAME GYM

REAL HUMAN BEINGS ONLY!

TICKETS: $10

"Stop!" someone shouted. Coming toward them, pushing her special thirty-six-inch Thunderwear®™ Power Push Sweet Sweep Fine Bristle Push Broom,[27] was the school's gold-medal custodian, Olga Shotput.

"You must have written permission from a principal to put posters on the walls," Olga said. "Show me your permission slip."

"But these posters support REAL human beings," said Fibby.

"It doesn't matter," said Olga. "The school's rules say you must have written permission."

"If you don't let us put up these posters, you're being pro-mythology," Fibby said.

---

[27] See *Is That an Angry Penguin in Your Gym Bag?* for more information on this remarkable and versatile broom.

"I would never be pro-mythology," Olga said. "I am merely following the school's rules."

"Then the school's rules are pro-mythology," said Fibby. "And if you follow pro-mythology rules, that makes *you* pro-mythology. And *that* means you'll have to give up your gold medal in custodianship because there are no gold medals for custodianship in mythology."

Olga shrank back fearfully. "No, no! I'm not pro-mythology, I swear! For many years I worked and struggled to earn my gold medal in custodianship, which I finally won in the fourth book of this fabulous and exalted series."

"If you try to stop us from putting up these posters I will have no choice but to inform the National Committee for

Custodial Olympics of your pro-mythology activities," Fibby threatened.

"Oh, look! I see dirt on the floor at the far end of the hall!" Olga declared. "Dirt is pro-mythology and I hate everything pro-mythology and therefore I hate dirt." She quickly began to push her broom away.

Fibby turned to her mother. "You may continue putting up the posters."

THE
END OF
BARRY
THE
BACTERIA

At lunchtime the Tardy Boys and their friends went to the cafeteria. As they approached the school lobby, the BRATA-RATA-BRATA-RATA! sound grew louder and louder and the building shook more and more. The lobby was filled with construction workers smashing through the floor with jackhammers and pickaxes. Nearby, the APOKS stood wearing his yellow foam earplugs, white breathing mask, and blue latex gloves.

As the Tardy Boys and their friends passed, each of them had different thoughts. Thanks to the Jumbo Atomic Omnitron, you, the reader, can now know what each of them is thinking:

1) The author is upset that Leyton blames him for having no ideas when it was almost certainly the Arthur who'd told the teensy-weensy brain cells to hitch rides to the beach for National Tooth Fairy Day.

2) Wade is wondering why the United Thunderwear®™ Corporation would want to donate a Fountain of Cleanliness to The School With No Name.

3) Daisy is worried that if Fibby is allowed to turn St. Patrick's Day into the Feast of the Millionaire Nun, she might next decide to change Christmas into The Whole World Showers Fibby Mandible with Expensive Gifts Day.

4) Leyton is wondering if the author could be so incredibly mean and cruel that he was going to let his brain cells take off that day, National Pig Day, as well.

5) The Jumbo Atomic Omnitron still can't see through Velostat Thought-Screen Helmets. However, it would guess that Al-Ian is still yearning for The One Who Caused His Heart to Flutter ♥.

6) There is one other mind that the Jumbo Atomic Omnitron can see

into. It is an ultra-teensy-weensy mind. So small that one of Leyton's itsy-bitsy brain cells would look like a huge mountain next to it. This is the mind of Barry the Bacteria.

a. Barry is a friendly bacteria of the type known as *Lactobacillus acidophilus*. One of the things Barry likes to do is make yogurt. In fact, it is almost impossible to make yogurt without Barry's help. It makes Barry feel good to know that so many people around the world enjoy the work he does.

b. On this particular day, Barry is on a counter in the kitchen of The School With No Name. Barry isn't sure how he got there, but when you're a bacteria, stuff like this happens. Barry figures he'll just have to wait until something changes and he gets to make yogurt again.

c. What Barry doesn't figure on is looking up and seeing a person wearing a black Thunderwear®™ jumpsuit enter the kitchen carrying a huge spray bottle filled with Thunderwear®™ Germ-Massacring Spray Disinfectant!

d. Rest in peace, Barry.

When the Tardy Boys and their friends got to the cafeteria, they noticed something strange — no one was eating. And then they saw why. The doors to the kitchen were chained shut. A sign hanging from the chain read:

CLOSED UNTIL FURTHER NOTICE

Just then, a familiar-looking assistant principal strolled past.

"Excuse me, Assistant Principal Snout?" Daisy said.

The assistant principal did not respond.

"Assistant Principal Snout?" Daisy said more loudly to get his attention, but the assistant principal still did not respond.

Daisy took off her rose-colored granny glasses. She took a deep breath and was about to yell when Wade stopped her. "He's not Assistant Principal Snout anymore, remember? His identity was stolen."

Daisy's mouth fell open. "You're right! I forgot. Excuse me, Assistant Principal Once Known as Snout."

The APOKS turned. "Yes, Daisy?"

"Why is the kitchen closed?" Daisy asked.

"Because we've discovered something shocking," answered the APOKS. "There are bacteria in there."

"So?" said Al-Ian.

"So how can we call ourselves a National Blue Ribbon Germfree School if we've got germs in our kitchen?" replied the APOKS.

"As we've tried to tell you many times before, there are billions and billions of germs everywhere," said Daisy. "And many of them are good germs. We need germs in our bodies to help with digestion. Without bacteria, we wouldn't have cheese and yogurt. Bacteria are needed to break down dead plants and animals to create the soil we need to grow food. Without bacteria, life on this planet couldn't exist."[28]

"We'll see about that," grumbled the APOKS. "Right now the Thunderwear®™ Germ Destruction Team is in there killing every germ in sight."

"What are we supposed to do about lunch?" asked Al-Ian.

"Don't bother," said the APOKS.

"But we're hungry," said Wade.

"So?" said the APOKS. "Lots of people get hungry. Look around the cafeteria. It's filled with hungry kids. You don't hear them complaining, do you?"

"Hey, we're hungry!" complained a kid at a table nearby.

"Yeah, what are we supposed to eat?" complained someone else.

---

[28] True that, homey.

"This is no fair!" complained a third. "We need food!"

"How come I didn't get any roast beef?" cried something that resembled a freshly washed toe.[29]

The APOKS ignored them.

"Why are you ignoring them?" asked Daisy.

"Because if I ignore them, they might go away," said the APOKS.

Just then the doors to the cafeteria opened and Ulna Mandible rushed in, followed by Fibby. When Ulna saw the APOKS she screamed, *"Have you gone insane?"*

---

[29] This little toe note had none.

KA-BOING!

The APOKS pretended that he didn't hear her. Ulna Mandible rushed up to him. "*Are you ignoring me?*" she shrieked.

The APOKS slowly turned and looked at her as if he'd never seen her before. "I'm sorry, but I think you must be mistaken."

"*What are you talking about?*" Ulna bellowed.

"I suspect you are looking for Assistant

Principal Snout," said the APOKS. "But his identity has been stolen."

"*Then who are you?*" Ulna screeched.

"I am the Assistant Principal Once Known as Snout," he said.

"*I see!*" screamed Ulna. "*Well, I suppose I'll just have to look for him somewhere else. Come, Fibby, let's go find the REAL Assistant Principal Snout.*"

Fibby and her mother left the cafeteria.

"It worked!" Al-Ian gasped.

"I can't believe they actually fell for it!" Daisy cried.

The APOKS smiled broadly. Suddenly a cell phone in his pocket began to ring. The APOKS answered it. "Hello? Yes, this is that phone number. Yes, I guess the person who owns this phone would be the one who'd answer it. Well, I suppose you're right about that."

The smile left the APOKS's face and he turned pale with fear. Across the cafeteria the doors swung open again and Ulna Mandible marched in, holding a cell phone to her ear. "So, *do you still insist that you're not Assistant Principal Snout?*" she hollered.

"I'm sure I could take a message for him," said the APOKS.

"*Fine!*" screamed Ulna. "*You can tell him that he's in big trouble because now that he's closed the school kitchen we have no way to prepare the food for the Feast of the Millionaire Nun.*"

"I'll tell him," said the APOKS.

"*And tell him that if he doesn't figure out a way to have the Feast of the Millionaire Nun, the United Thunderwear®™ Corporation just might decide to take back the Fountain of Cleanliness!*" Ulna screamed.

"Oh! That would be terrible!" cried the APOKS. "I'll be sure to tell him that."

Once again, Ulna and Fibby stormed out of the cafeteria. The APOKS slumped down at a table and held his head in his hands, but not under his arm like a Dullahan would.

"What is the Assistant Principal Once Known as Snout going to do?" he moaned woefully.

The Tardy Boys and their friends sat down with him. Despite the fact that he punished them more than any other students at school, they felt bad for him. It wasn't easy to be constantly harassed by irate and unreasonable parents. It wasn't easy to live at school 24/7 because you couldn't function in the real world. It wasn't easy to stand on one foot and jump up and down while you rubbed your tummy and patted your head.

The Jumbo Atomic Omnitron will now show you, the reader, what the Tardy Boys and their friends are thinking while they sit at the table with the APOKS:

1) The APOKS is wondering if he now has to stand on one foot and jump up and down while he rubs his tummy and pats his head just because the author wrote that.

2) The author is certain that it was the Arthur who told Leyton's brain cells to take off that day, National Pig Day, as well. And at that very moment many of those cells are on a bus to the pig farm. But that didn't mean he, the author, can't write

that a few of them have overslept
and missed the bus.

3) Wade and Daisy are wondering
   how they will make it through the
   rest of the day without eating.

4) The Jumbo Atomic Omnitron
   guesses that Al-Ian is wondering
   if The Girl Who Caused His Heart
   to Flutter ♥ likes him as much as
   he likes her.

5) Leyton is wondering why it
   suddenly feels like a few of
   his brains cells have overslept
   and missed the bus to the
   pig farm. He closes his eyes and
   concentrates very hard. If there
   really are any teensy-weensy
   brain cells still asleep in his
   skull, they will start to wake. They
   will yawn and rub their teensy-

weensy brain cell eyes and stretch their itsy-bitsy brain cell arms. They may pull on robes and slippers and shuffle into the kitchen and make coffee. Or they may shower and dress and drive to the closest Starbucks.

But nothing like that happened. Leyton decided that he had to concentrate even harder. He squeezed his eyes more tightly and balled his hands into fists and gritted his teeth.

"What are you doing?" Wade asked.

"Concentrating," Leyton answered.

"Why?" asked Wade.

"To see if any of my brain cells have overslept and missed the bus to the pig farm."

When Wade heard that, he gave his brother *The Look*.

Leyton hated *The Look*. He hated it more than he hated The Awful Fate of Flunkdom. More than he hated snirt.[30] Even more than he hated authors who told his brain cells to take off *two days in a row!* Leyton hated *The Look* so much that he decided to have an idea *whether or not his brain cells were even there!*

Leyton gritted his teeth harder and clenched his fists tighter. He concentrated so hard that if his head had been a jar, the top would have spun off. So hard that if his skull had been a cherry bomb, it would have exploded. So hard that if he'd

---

[30] See *Is That a Sick Cat in Your Backpack?* for more information on this unique and remarkable substance.

had water on the brain, steam would
have come out of his ears!

He concentrated and concentrated
and . . .

Ka-boing! Into his head popped a big,
happy, fuzzy, glowing IDEA.

Leyton turned to the sad and miserable
APOKS and said, "I have the answer to
your problem."

The APOKS looked stunned. "What is it?"

"You can still have the feast," said
Leyton. "Only instead of cooking food
here, we'll bring it from home."

"Bring Your Own Barbecue!" Wade cried.

A REALLY BIG BRING YOUR OWN BARBECUE!

Everyone agreed that Leyton's idea was brilliant and that probably not all his brain cells had taken the bus to the pig farm for National Pig Day. After not eating lunch, the Tardy Boys and their friends went to their classes and tried to learn despite the grumbling in their empty tummies and the loud BRATA-RATA-BRATA-RATA! of construction workers' jackhammers.

When it was time for gym they discovered that bright yellow DO NOT CROSS tape was blocking the entrance to the locker rooms.

"Why can't we go into the locker rooms?" Wade asked Mr. Braun, the gym teacher who had replaced Mr. Circle in Book Four of this extraordinary series.

"Because we're watching a video today," replied Mr. Braun. "It's called *The Dangers of Exercise* and was sent to us by the American Television Association."

"But isn't gym class where kids are supposed to exercise?" asked 3-M.

"Not anymore," said Mr. Braun. "There's too much potential for injuries. Did you know that kids are four times more likely to be injured playing sports than sitting at home watching TV?"

"If we can't get exercise, can we at least go outside?" asked Daisy.

Mr. Braun shook his head. "No way. It's much too dangerous outside."

"Because there's a risk of being kidnapped by aliens?" Al-Ian guessed.

"No," said Mr. Braun.

"Because of the photochemical pollution?" asked Daisy.

"No," said the gym teacher. "It's because of the barbecue pit. Now sit down and stop asking me questions." He went into the gym office, leaving the Tardy Boys and their friends with lots of unasked questions. But thanks to the Jumbo Atomic Omnitron, you, the reader, can learn what those questions are:

1) Wade wants to ask if a barbecue pit is like a tar pit, but instead of being

filled with subterranean bitumen (asphalt), it is filled with barbecue sauce.

2) Leyton is wondering whether a barbecue pit could be larger than a double coconut palm pit, which might weigh up to 60 pounds and is universally considered the world's largest pit.

3) The author is wondering if Leyton will blame him for whatever cruel and nasty trick the Arthur will play next.

4) The Jumbo Atomic Omnitron can only guess that Al-Ian wants to know if The Love of His Young Life ♥ would agree to hold his hand.

5) Daisy wants to know why a barbecue pit means they can't go outside. The only way to get the

answer, she decides, is to go to
the window and look.

"Where are you going?" Wade asked.

"To the window to see why a barbecue
pit would stop us from going outside,"
said Daisy. She went to the window and
gasped. "Oh my gosh!"

The Tardy Boys and Al-Ian rushed to see
what had made Daisy gasp.

Outside, three bright yellow backhoes
were digging a huge hole in the athletic
field, and bright yellow dump trucks were
hauling the earth away.

"That's going to be some barbecue pit,"
said Wade.

"Way bigger than a double coconut
palm pit," said Leyton.

"Why in the world would they need a
pit that big?" wondered Al-Ian.

"Maybe they want to grow a really big barbecue," said Leyton.

"I'd like to know why all that construction equipment says United Thunderwear®™ Corporation on it," said Daisy.[31]

---

[31] This little toe note cried, "Wee wee wee," all the way home.

LOVE CONQUERS 20 MULE TEAM BORAX

When school ended, the Tardy Boys and their friends met 3-M and Brendan in the school lobby.

"How's ESL class?" Daisy asked 3-M.

"It's silly," 3-M complained. "My English is as good as everyone else's. If they won't put me into the regular classes, I may have to transfer to another school."

Hearing those words, Al-Ian felt as if a knife had just pierced his heart! As if he'd just been tossed into the abyss! No, he told himself. *That can't happen! I won't let it!*

By now the construction workers had torn up the lobby floor and were busy digging a big hole for the Fountain of Cleanliness. Outside, parked at the curb in front of the school under the hazy gray photochemically polluted sky, were trucks from the United Thunderwear®™ Corporation.

As the Tardy Boys and their friends walked home, they began to see signs stuck in lawns saying:

CELEBRATE

THE FEAST OF THE MILLIONAIRE NUN

(AND NOT THAT OTHER HOLIDAY)

ON MARCH 17

AT THE SCHOOL WITH NO NAME

REAL HUMAN BEINGS ONLY!

BRING YOUR OWN BARBECUE

Then they heard the high-pitched whine of Barton's shiny new BladeX motorized scooter as he rode toward them. Hanging from his neck was a bright green MP3 player connected to earphones over his ears.

Barton stopped the scooter, pulled off the earphones, and quoted Euripides,[32] "Love distills desire upon the eyes, love brings bewitching grace into the heart."

------

[32] Greek playwright, left fielder, and switch hitter on the Athens Angels. He is not related to Euripides Pants and his brother Eusewidies Pants, who were both tailors.

"I'm amazed at how much love poetry you know!" Daisy gasped.

Barton smiled, got back on his scooter, and drove away.

"Now he's got the Green Bean pPod MP3 player," Wade grumbled. "I read that it's the most expensive MP3 player made."

"Something's not right," said Al-Ian.

"Something other than a left, a wrong, a humpback, or a minke?" Leyton asked.

"Yes," said Al-Ian. "Where did Barton get the money for that scooter and MP3 player? And why will the Fountain of Cleanliness spout Thunderwear®™ Deluxe Crystal-Clear Germ-Massacring Hand Sanitizer? And why is the United Thunderwear®™ Corporation digging around the school? And why do they only want REAL humans at the Feast of the Millionaire Nun?"

"We already know from Book Four in this widely wild and readily read series that Fibby's father, Sternum Mandible, owns and operates the United Thunderwear®™ Corporation," Wade realized.

"Do you think building the Fountain of Cleanliness and digging the giant barbecue pit and Brendan's missing pot of gold are all tied together?" 3-M asked.

Now that Leyton knew for certain that not all of his brain cells were taking off National Pig Day, he tried to think of how the construction trucks and the fountain and the Feast of the Millionaire Nun and a missing pot of gold could all be tied together. It didn't seem possible that anyone had a piece of rope *that* long. To try to figure out the answer, all the itsy-bitsy teensy-weensy brain cells who'd missed the bus to the pig farm that morning stretched a trampoline across the inside of his skull and began to bounce up and down. They bounced higher and higher until . . . *Ka-boing!* Leyton had a realization. All those things weren't really tied together with rope!

"It's another idiom!" he shouted.

"That's right!" Wade patted him on the back.

"You figured it out!" Daisy said happily.

Leyton grinned proudly. All the itsy-bitsy brain cells in his skull stopped bouncing and started to cheer.

"But, idiomatically speaking, how can it all be tied together?" asked Wade. "What does building a giant Fountain of Cleanliness in the lobby of our school have to do with digging up the athletic field and turning it into a giant barbecue pit? And what could those things have to do with

Brendan never getting his pot of gold back and spending the rest of his life being the only clinically depressed little pointy-eared mythological being of Irish descent on record? And what could any of that have to do with making the Feast of the Millionaire Nun for REAL humans only?"

Leyton waited for the teensy-itsy-weensy-bitsy brain cells in his skull to get back on the trampoline and start bouncing again, but the brain cells all stood around shaking their weensy-teensy heads. They were exhausted from helping Leyton figure out that last idiom and needed to take a rest.

"That's a hard question to answer," said Leyton.

"Really hard," agreed 3-M.

They turned and looked at Al-Ian, who was a certified member of the National

Association of Brainiacs. Al-Ian thought it would be hard to tie all those things together. But then he looked into 3-M's eyes and suddenly he knew that no matter how big and difficult the problem was, it could be solved because Love Conquers All ♥. He had also heard that Love Conquers Tide, Cheer, Wisk, and 20 Mule Team Borax.[33] Al-Ian believed that as long as he had His Dearest Most Cherished One ♥ by his side, he could do anything.

"I can do anything," Al-Ian said.

"Can you figure out what Fibby and her parents are up to?" asked Daisy.

"I'll work on it," said Al-Ian.

---

[33] A laundry detergent known for more than a hundred years around the world as the essential laundry booster and multipurpose cleaner.

THE COINCIDENCE
OF INTERTWINGULATION

The next morning the Tardy Boys, Daisy,
3-M, and Brendan walked to school. When
they got to the corner where they usually
met Al-Ian, he wasn't there.

"I wonder what could have happened to
him," said Daisy.

"I'll call." 3-M took out her red Swiss
Army BlackBerry and called Al-Ian. She
spoke to him for a few moments and then

hung up. "He was up all night trying to figure out the answer to that question, and now he's too tired to go to school. He said he'll see us at lunch."

"Did he figure out the answer?" asked Wade.

"No," said 3-M. "He says he won't know the answer until the author writes the next chapter in this book."

Typical mean author trick, Leyton thought bitterly.

So the Tardy Boys and their friends minus Al-Ian continued to school. When they got there, workers from the United Thunderwear®™ Corporation were busy digging holes everywhere — in the school lawn, in the sidewalk, and in the parking lot.

"Why are they digging all these holes?" 3-M asked.

"I'm not sure," said Daisy. "But I bet it has to do with the Feast of the Millionaire Nun."

"That makes perfect sense," said Leyton. "Fibby wants it to be a holy day."

Wade and Daisy and the others stared at him with their mouths agape.

"That's amazing!" Daisy gasped.

"You mean because I was right?" asked Leyton.

"No, because you were *funny*," said Wade.

Leyton grinned with great pride and thought, *I forgive you, Mr. Author.*

As usual when the Tardy Boys and their friends arrived at school, Fibby and Ulna Mandible were already there. The APOKS was also there. But Ulna was not shouting, yelling, screaming, screeching, and shrieking at him. She wasn't even hollering or bellowing. In fact, nary[34] a sound came from her lips.

"Why isn't your mother shouting, yelling, screaming, screeching, shrieking, hollering, or bellowing?" Wade asked Fibby.

"She has no one to shout, yell, scream, screech, shriek, holler, or bellow at," said Fibby. "The only one here is this very nice gentleman who is pretending not to be Assistant Principal Snout."

"But I thought your mother was furious

---

[34] Strange word, but not nearly as strange as the narwhal, which comes right before it in the dictionary. Narwhals have a unicornlike tusk. For more information on this remarkable whale, take a swim in the Arctic Ocean.

at him because he closed the school kitchen," said Daisy.

"That was before he told us to have everyone bring barbecue from home," said Fibby. "Now my mom and I don't have to worry about cooking for the Feast of the Millionaire Nun. We're going to start the feast with a bang."

"Why are workers for your father's company digging holes all over the place?" asked Daisy.

"In honor of the Feast of the Millionaire Nun, my father has decided to donate five hundred trees to the school," Fibby said.

The bell rang and the Tardy Boys and their friends went into school.

"It seems like Fibby's family is finding lots of reasons for digging holes all over the school," Daisy said.

Suddenly Leyton saw an opportunity to be funny again. "Maybe the author is making them do it so that he can call this book *Holes*!"

Everyone groaned.

"Oh, come on," Leyton said. "That was funny."

"No, it wasn't," said 3-M.

Leyton grit his teeth and thought, *Once again, I hate you, Mr. Author!*

Inside The School With No Name, workers wearing black Thunderwear®™ jumpsuits were digging up the floors of classrooms. Ms. Fitt came down the hall pushing a wheelbarrow filled with books.

"Why are they digging up the classrooms, Ms. Fitt?" Daisy asked.

"They're putting in underground wiring for the new video projection system," Ms.

Fitt said. "This is so exciting! Now I can get rid of the rest of these old books. Do you realize that once this project is finished, The School With No Name will be the first Blue Ribbon Completely Bookless School in the whole country?!"

"Is that a good thing?" asked 3-M.

"Of course it is," said Ms. Fitt. "Think of how much room these books take up. Now we'll be able to fill all that space with DVDs."

She hurried away, pushing the wheelbarrow of books ahead of her.

"This is crazy," said Daisy. "First they started digging up the school lobby for the Fountain of Cleanliness. Then they started digging up the athletic field for a giant barbecue pit. Then they started digging up the lawn and parking lot so they could plant trees. Now they're digging up all the classrooms."

"Do you think they're looking for something?" asked Wade.

"Whatever they're looking for must be pretty valuable if it's worth digging up the whole school for," said 3-M.

Now that they'd had time to rest, the refreshed and relaxed itsy-teensy-bitsy-weensy brain cells in Leyton's skull who'd missed the bus to the pig farm climbed back on the trampoline and started to bounce again. The question was: What could Fibby and her family be looking for?

People usually looked for things that were missing or lost.

Leyton glanced at Brendan. The little pointy-eared mythological person of Irish descent looked sad because he'd lost his pot of gold.

Leyton had to admit that it was kind of ironic that Fibby and her family were so busy looking for something really valuable, and at the same time, Brendan had lost something really valuable. There was a word for things like that.

"Intertwingled," Leyton said.

"What?" said Daisy.

"Intertwingled," said Leyton. "It's when two things happen at the same time just by chance and they're kind of related to each other and it's sort of a surprise."

"That's funny," said 3-M, "because the word *coincidence* means the same thing."

"What did you find so coincidentally intertwingled?" asked Daisy.

"That's the thing," said Leyton.

"What's The Thing?" asked Wade.

"A really scary movie[35] about an alien you never, ever want to meet," said 3-M.

"That's The Thing?" said Daisy.

"No, that's a different thing," said Leyton. "This thing is the intertwingulation of the coincidentalation."

"And what would that be?" asked Wade.

"That Fibby and her family are so busy looking for something really valuable, and at the same time, Brendan has lost something really valuable," said Leyton.

"You're right, Leyton," said Daisy. "That does sound like a coincidence."

"I'm hungry," said Wade.

---

[35] Originally called *The Thing from Another World*, this movie scared the socks off the author.

"Me, too," said 3-M. "I wish the cafeteria wasn't closed."

"I bet we could get some granola bars from the candy machine," said Daisy.

"Good idea," said Wade.

"What about the coincidence of intertwingulation?" asked Leyton.

"We'll talk about it later," answered Daisy.

Leyton clenched his fists angrily. *I know who made her say that! You, Mr. Author!*

MR. JUMBO
ATOMIC
OMNITRON
SPEAKS

(We now take you to an interview with
Mr. Jumbo Atomic Omnitron, well-known
mind reader.)

The author: May I call you Jumbo?
Jumbo: Yes, that's fine. Thank you for
having me here today.
The author: Well, Jumbo, the first thing
I would like to know is, why is Leyton

blaming me for all those things when they are obviously the Arthur's fault?

Jumbo: Wait a minute. I thought you were the Arthur.

The author: No, I'm the author.

Jumbo: Then who's the Arthur?

The author: I thought you knew.

Jumbo: No way, José.

The author: What's José got to do with this?

Jumbo: Listen, I don't have time for this. I'm a busy Atomic Omnitron. Now what else do you want to know?

The author: I think our readers would like to know who Brendan really is and where he came from.

Jumbo: Brendan is a mythological being known as a leprechaun. He comes from the island of Ireland.

The author: One assumes from reading this story that he is here because he's looking for his pot of gold?

Jumbo: Yes. Pots of gold are usually found at the ends of rainbows, but photochemical smog stops rainbows from occurring. When Brendan looked for his pot of gold after a prolonged period of photochemical smog, he discovered that it was missing.

The author: Obviously he believes his pot of gold is now somewhere in this story. What led him to believe this?

Jumbo: Certain top secret government agencies were involved in gathering that information. I could tell you more, but then I'd have to kill you.

The author: Just one more. Why did the leprechaun cross the road?

Jumbo: That's it. You're toast.

THE
ARTHUR
ARRIVES

Many days passed, including What If Cats and Dogs Had Opposable Thumbs? Day, Check Your Batteries Day, and Lips Appreciation Day. Nowhere among those days was there one called the United Thunderwear®™ Corporation Digs Up Every Square Inch of School Property Day, but that did not stop them from doing just that.

"I can't believe we have to stand in the

swimming pool," Daisy complained
the day before the Feast of the
Millionaire Nun.

"It's a good thing there's no water in it
or we'd be really cold," said Al-Ian.

"It's a good thing this pool is really big
or we'd be squashed," said 3-M.

"Why do they want us to stand in the
swimming pool anyway?" asked Leyton.

"Because it's the only place on school
property where they haven't dug,"
said Wade.

Just then Barton strolled by wearing
a brand-new pair of Yike Gold-plated Air
Cushions, the most expensive sneakers
in the world. He quoted John Keats,[36]

------

[36] In 1816 this English poet and catcher for
the London Lox reached base safely in forty-
seven straight games.

"Two souls with but a single thought, two hearts that beat as one."

"Oh, Barton!" Daisy gushed.

Barton handed a sheet of paper to the Tardy Boys and their friends.

THE FEAST OF THE MILLIONAIRE NUN IS AN

ALL-AMERICAN EVENT

FOR REAL HUMANS ONLY!

NO MYTHOLOGICAL BEINGS WILL BE ALLOWED

ESPECIALLY LITTLE POINTY-EARED MYTHOLOGICAL

BEINGS FROM IRELAND

Then the bell rang and it was time for all the students to climb out of the swimming pool and go home.

On the way home, Wade said, "I still don't understand how Barton can afford a brand-new BladeX scooter, a Green Bean pPod, and Yike Gold-plated Air

Cushions. It's not like anyone has found the pot of gold. So where did he get all that money?"

Al-Ian pointed down the street. "There's Mr. Roy and Wheezy. Let's ask him."

Mr. Roy was a huge, muscular man with arms as thick as car tires and legs like tree trunks. He was a professional wrestler and had scars on his face and a bent nose that looked like it had been broken twenty times. He was wearing black nylon shorts, a black hoodie, and sneakers, and carried a small, very smelly pug dog.[37]

---

[37] See *Is That a Dead Dog in Your Locker?* for more information about this remarkably smelly little dog.

The Tardy Boys and their friends said hello to him and then asked if he knew how Barton could afford so many expensive things.

"That's easy," said Mr. Roy. When he spoke you could see the gaps where he was missing teeth. "He borrowed money from Hammerhead Charlie, the loan shark."

"Sharks lend money?" said Leyton.

"Only loan sharks," said Mr. Roy.

"Are loan sharks lone sharks?" asked Al-Ian.

"No. Some work in pairs," said Mr. Roy.

"Do they also work in apples?" asked Leyton.

"Only when they're home alone," said Mr. Roy.

"So loan sharks are only lone sharks when they're alone at home?" asked 3-M.

"Yes," said Mr. Roy.

"But why would Hammerhead Charlie lend Barton money?" asked Daisy.

"Because Barton said he would pay him back with interest when he found the gold," said Mr. Roy.

"What if Barton loses interest?" asked 3-M.

"Then Hammerhead will put the bite on him," said Mr. Roy.

"Yikes," said Wade.

Mr. Roy looked down at his sneakers. "No, Addidas."

Mr. Roy continued on his way, and the Tardy Boys and their friends went home.

"Something smells fishy," said Daisy.

"That's an idiom!" cried Leyton.

"I think we should all go to your house and put our heads together," said 3-M.

"Another idiom!" cried Leyton.

"If we do, we should be able to get to the bottom of this," said Al-Ian.

"Yet another idiom!" cried Leyton.

Daisy sighed. "Leyton, we know they're idioms. And we're happy that *you* know they're idioms. But we'd really appreciate it if you'd stop reminding us each time we use one."

"Can I point out *some* idioms?" Leyton asked.

"No," said Daisy.

"How about rare idioms?" Leyton asked.

"Not that, either."

I'll get you for this, Mr. Author, Leyton thought angrily.

As they continued home, something small and toelike ran past crying, "Wee wee wee," but the Tardy Boys and their friends were too lost in thought to notice. Later, in the house, they sat around the kitchen table trying to think of an answer.

They sat and thought.

And thought and sat.

"At this rate, we're never going to figure out what's going on," Al-Ian complained.

"How come authors always know what's going to happen next and we don't?" asked Leyton.

"Sometimes they have a Jumbo Atomic Omnitron," said Al-Ian.

"I wish we had a Jumbo Atomic Omnitron," said Daisy. "Then we'd be able to figure everything out, too."

Just then there was a knock on the door. Wade said, "Go see who it is, Leyton."

"No way," said Leyton. "You're not the boss of me and you're not eating soggy Chocolate Lucky Charms, either."

Wade gave Leyton *The Look*, and Leyton gave Wade *The Look Right Back*.

"I'll go see who it is," said TJ. He went to the door and then came back. "It's someone called Arthur and he wants to speak to Daisy."

Daisy frowned and went to see who this Arthur person was. The others waited in the kitchen.

And waited and sat.

And sat and waited.

Finally Wade went to the kitchen window and looked outside.

"See anything?" Al-Ian asked.

"Just a big truck with the words Mobile Jumbo Atomic Omnitron painted on the side," said Wade.

A few moments later Daisy rushed back into the kitchen. "It has nothing to do with whether or not we're REAL humans!" she said excitedly. "That's just an excuse Fibby made up to keep Brendan away from the Feast of the Millionaire Nun so he can't claim his pot of gold when they find it!"

"But how are they going to find it?" asked Wade. "They've already dug up the whole school."

"The United Thunderwear®™ Corporation has just brought a Not-So-Secret Weapon to school that will help them find it," Daisy said.

Al-Ian jumped to his feet. "Come on! We've got to go see what that Not-So-Secret Weapon is!"

THE NOT-SO-SECRET WEAPON

By now it was getting dark. The Tardy Boys and their friends snuck into the school parking lot. A big flatbed trailer was parked near the fence. On it something very large was hidden under an enormous black tarp.

"Why do I think that's the Not-So-Secret Weapon?" Al-Ian whispered.

"Maybe because those words are stenciled in big white letters on the tarp?" Wade said.

NOT-SO-SECRET WEAPON:
THUNDERWEAR®™ WEATHER MODIFICATION SERVICE

"Let's see what's under it," said Wade.

The Tardy Boys and their friends lifted a corner of the tarp and peeked under. 3-M switched on the flashlight in her Swiss Army BlackBerry. The thing under the tarp had two ginormous tires. Above the tires was a huge, round, metal tube as long as a flagpole, but much thicker.

"What is it?" 3-M whispered.

"I think it's some kind of machine," whispered Wade.

Leyton found some white letters stenciled to the metal tube. "Hey, check this out! It says 'Super Anti-aircraft Cannon.'"

"What in the world would they need a cannon this big for?" 3-M wondered.

"Maybe they want to shoot someone out of it," Leyton said.

"I don't think so," said Wade. "This thing is huge. If they shot you out of it, you'd probably land on some planet out in the solar system."

"Like on Neptune?" asked Daisy.

"Or even on Uranus," said TJ.

"Maybe they plan to shoot down alien spaceships!" Al-Ian gasped.

"But why would it say weather modification service?" Daisy asked.

"Maybe it's just a cover-up," said Al-Ian.

"Of course it's a cover-up," said Wade. "That's what tarps do."

"No, no, I meant the weather modification part," Al-Ian said. "They can't go around towing a giant anti-aircraft gun with 'For Blowing UFOs Out of the Sky' printed on the side, so they call it weather modification instead."

Leyton had wandered off toward the back of the flatbed trailer. Now he returned. "You guys should check out the giant bullet," he said.

"You mean 'shell'?" Al-Ian gasped.

Leyton shook his head. "Not a shell. A really big bullet."

"Dude, a shell is what they call a really big bullet," Wade said.

"No way," said Leyton. "A shell is what a mollusk, a turtle, or an armadillo has for protection. Believe me, there was no mollusk, turtle, or armadillo living in the thing I just saw."

But no one was listening. They'd all hurried to the back of the flatbed trailer to look at the shell.

"Wow, it's huge!" Wade gasped.

3-M shined her flashlight on it. "It says silver iodide."

"What's that?" asked Al-Ian.

3-M Googled it on her Swiss Army BlackBerry. "Silver iodide[38] is a chemical compound used in photography and for cloud seeding."

---

[38] Silver iodide is the combination of one atom of silver and one atom of iodine. It is a real substance and was used by Poison Ivy to introduce a new breed of plants to Gotham City.

"Why would anyone want to seed a cloud?" asked Al-Ian.

"Because sometimes they're really pretty," said Leyton.

"Huh?" said Wade.

"You know, like around sunset when they get all pink and orange and purple," Leyton explained. "Haven't you ever seed a pretty cloud?"

"You mean, *seen* a cloud?" said Daisy.

"Maybe you've seen them," said Leyton. "But I've seed them."

"You didn't *seed* them, you *saw* them," said Al-Ian.

"You can't saw a cloud," said Leyton. "They're not made of wood. They're either made of photochemical pollution or water vapor."

"Oh my gosh! That's it!" Daisy gasped.

A REALLY
BIG
BANG

"I just figured out Fibby's plan," Daisy said. "She's going to use the huge cannon to fire that giant shell filled with silver iodide into the clouds to seed them!"

"Why?" asked Wade.

"Because when you seed a cloud, you make it rain," Daisy said. "And once you've drained all the water vapor out of a cloud it goes away and then the sun comes out."

"You mean that big, round, hot, yellow thing in the sky?" Leyton said.

"Yes," said Daisy.

"It's nice of Fibby to do that," said Leyton. "I think people have really missed seeing the sun."

"But that's not why she's doing it," said Daisy. "What happens when the sun comes out and dries up all the rain?"

"The itsy-bitsy spider goes up the spout again," said Leyton.

"No!" 3-M realized. "There's a rainbow!"

"What about the itsy-bitsy spider?" said Leyton.

"Dude, what's at the end of a rainbow?" Wade asked.

"The letter *w*," said Leyton.

"No," said Daisy. "At the end of a rainbow is . . . a pot of gold."

"You're right!" Al-Ian cried.

"Remember Fibby said they'd start the feast with a bang?" Wade said. "I bet she meant the bang from firing that giant silver iodide shell into the clouds."

"And as soon as that rainbow comes out they'll find the pot of gold," said Daisy.

"Unless we find it first," said Al-Ian.

"And get to keep all the gold for ourselves!" said Leyton.

"No, dude, we'll give it to Brendan," said Wade.

"Why?" asked Leyton.

"Because I'm really tired of having a bummed-out little pointy-eared mythological being of Irish descent hanging around the house all day," said Wade.

"Yeah, it is kind of a drag," said TJ. "And his pipe smells yucky."

"We have to get Brendan into school tomorrow so he can claim his gold," Daisy said.

"But we can't," said Al-Ian. "He's not allowed to come to the Feast of the Millionaire Nun because he's not a REAL human."

"Then we'll sneak him in," said Wade.

AT THE
BOTTOM
OF A
BIG HOLE

The next day the Tardy Boys and their friends headed for the Feast of the Millionaire Nun. Daisy and 3-M carried coleslaw and corn on the cob. Al-Ian and Wade carried potato salad and baked beans. Leyton pulled a wagon with a big plastic cooler in it.

When they got to The School With No Name it looked like a bomb had been dropped. Actually, it looked like many bombs had been dropped. There was hardly an inch of ground that had not been dug up. Fibby was standing at the school's entrance with people wearing black Thunderwear®™ jumpsuits.

"Check every bag and container!" Fibby ordered. "We have to be certain no mythological beings get in."

The Tardy Boys and their friends exchanged nervous looks and got in line. The people in the black Thunderwear®™ jumpsuits checked 3-M's coleslaw to make sure there were no mythological beings hiding in the carrots and cabbage. They checked the potato salad and baked beans, too.

Then it was Leyton's turn. With his heart banging nervously in his chest, he pulled the wagon up to the entrance.

"What's in that cooler?" Fibby asked.

"Barbecue," said Leyton.

Fibby narrowed her eyes suspiciously. "That's an awful big cooler. There must be a lot of barbecue in there."

Leyton began to tremble. "Enough to feed me and all my friends."

"I think I'd like to see just how much barbecue is really in there," Fibby said.

"But . . ." Leyton stammered.

"But what?" asked Fibby.

"Barbecue might be sleeping," said Leyton.

Fibby yanked the cooler open. Inside was a big platter of barbecue. Under the platter was ice to keep the barbecue cold.

Fibby pursed her lips. "Okay, you can go in."

The Tardy Boys and their friends went in. At the entrance to the gym, a person in a black Thunderwear®™ jumpsuit handed each of them a sheet of paper.

WELCOME TO THE VIDEO OF
THE FEAST OF THE MILLIONAIRE NUN
FOR REAL HUMANS ONLY

PLEASE NOTE THAT DUE TO RECENT CHANGES
IN SCHOOL POLICY, THE SCHOOL WITH NO
NAME IS NO LONGER ALLOWED TO HOLD FEASTS,
FESTIVALS, OR CELEBRATIONS ON SCHOOL
PROPERTY. THEREFORE, TODAY YOU WILL HAVE
THE PLEASURE OF WATCHING A VIDEO OF A FEAST.

THE SCHOOL WITH NO NAME WILL NOT BE
HELD RESPONSIBLE FOR ANY HARM CAUSED BY
WATCHING THIS VIDEO.

PLEASE NOTE THAT CHAIRS ARE FOR SITTING
ONLY. THE SCHOOL IS NOT RESPONSIBLE FOR
ANY HARM CAUSED BY THE MISUSE OF CHAIRS.

PLEASE SIT QUIETLY AND WATCH THE VIDEO.
THE SCHOOL IS NOT RESPONSIBLE FOR ANY
HARM CAUSED BY NOT SITTING QUIETLY AND
NOT WATCHING THE VIDEO.

PLEASE NOTE THAT YOU MAY BREATHE WHILE WATCHING THIS VIDEO. HOWEVER, THE SCHOOL WITH NO NAME IS NOT RESPONSIBLE FOR ANY HARM THAT MAY RESULT FROM BREATHING.

THANK YOU. PLEASE SIT BACK, RELAX, EAT YOUR BARBECUE, AND ENJOY THE VIDEO.

Many rows of chairs had been set up in the gym, and a giant screen hung at one end of the room.

"I don't know which is stranger," said 3-M, "the idea that we're supposed to *watch* a feast instead of *have* a feast. Or the idea that everyone in this gym seems to think that this is perfectly okay."

It was true. Everyone took their seats and waited for the video to begin.

"Notice who isn't here?" Daisy asked.

"How can you notice who isn't here?" Leyton asked. "Wouldn't someone have to be here for us to notice him?"

"Barton and Fibby and her mom," said Wade.

Soon the gym was filled to capacity. The lights went down and the video began. The Tardy Boys and their friends settled in to watch.

"I think there's something wrong with the sound," Al-Ian whispered after a few moments.

"Why?" asked Daisy.

"I keep hearing chattering noises," said Al-Ian.

"Oh my gosh!" gasped Daisy. "That's not the video! That's Brendan! We forgot about him! Get him out of the cooler, Leyton!"

Leyton quickly opened the cooler. He took out the platter of barbecue and then the shelf of ice under it. Under the shelf was a space where Brendan lay curled in a shivering ball. Even in the dark he looked more blue than green. The chattering of his teeth was so loud that the people sitting close by shushed him.

"Come on," Daisy whispered. "It's time to get out of here."

The Tardy Boys and their friends quietly got up and left the gym through a side door. Once they were outside, 3-M stopped and pointed. "Look!"

Out in the parking lot the tarp had been removed from the giant anti-aircraft cannon, and its huge barrel was aimed up toward the gray clouds of photochemical smog. People wearing black Thunderwear®™ jumpsuits were busy loading the giant shell. Then someone shouted "Duck!" and they all hurried away from the cannon and covered their ears.

Ker-pow! The huge cannon recoiled and coughed out a giant ball of smoke.

"Up there!" Al-Ian pointed skyward where a black speck was rocketing toward the gray photochemical clouds.

Ka-boom! There was a giant explosion as the giant shell filled with silver iodide blew up.

For a moment, everything was quiet. The people wearing the black Thunderwear®™ jumpsuits stared up at the gray sky. The Tardy Boys and their friends stared up at the gray sky. Somewhere someone named Arthur stared up at the gray sky.

"Maybe it won't work," said Al-Ian.

Crash! A bolt of lightning flashed. *Boom!* Thunder roared. Warm rain began to pour down and splash on the ground.

"It's like a waterfall!" Al-Ian shouted.

The people wearing the black Thunderwear®™ jumpsuits lowered the cannon and started to pull the tarp over it. Meanwhile, the pouring rain seeped into everyone's clothes, and puddles started to form on the ground.

"This is fun!" Daisy cried, running around and jumping in the puddles.

"Yeah! I can hardly remember the last time it rained!" shouted Wade.

Even Brendan seemed to enjoy the downpour. For a while everyone played in the rain and forgot about their problems. Then the rain gradually stopped and the air began to feel warm and moist.

"Look!" Wade pointed at the sky. A big, round, yellow ball appeared in the haze above them.

"The sun!" Al-Ian shouted.

"And look!" Daisy cried. A rainbow

began to stretch down toward the school. Brendan's mouth fell open and he started to run.

"Let's go!" 3-M shouted. The Tardy Boys and their friends followed Brendan toward the school. The rainbow seemed to go through the skylight over the lobby.

"Over there!" Daisy yelled. Ulna Mandible's big red Hummer skidded around the corner of the school and began to speed toward the front entrance. The Hummer screeched to a stop, and Ulna, Fibby, and Barton jumped out and raced in the front doors.

"They're going to get there first!" Al-Ian cried.

By the time the Tardy Boys and their friends got through the front doors, Fibby, her mother, and Barton had climbed down into the vast hole where the Fountain of Cleanliness was supposed to be built. The rainbow came down through the skylight and went right into the hole. The Tardy Boys and their friends got to the edge of the hole and looked down. At the bottom, bathed in ROY G. BIV,[39] Fibby was reaching into a big pot of glittering gold coins.

"Stop!" Wade shouted. "That's not yours!"

"It is too!" Fibby yelled back. "Under the General Mining Act of 1872, we are entitled to any gold we find!"

Ulna raised her hands in fists of victory. *"So it's all ours!"*

---

[39] Seventeenth-century scientist who invented color. Before color there was only black and white. Mr. Biv named each color after a letter in his name: Red, Orange, Yellow, Green, Blue, Indigo, and Violet.

SURPRISE

The Tardy Boys and their friends
glanced sadly at each other.

"It's over," 3-M said with a sorry sigh.

Wade hung his head woefully.

"This is so unfair!" Daisy cried angrily.

"And also not nice!" added Al-Ian
despondently.

Leyton looked at Brendan, thinking that

he would be the unhappiest of them all. But something was strange.

"Uh, guys?" said Leyton.

"Not now, Leyton," Daisy sniffed. "Can't you see that we are bemoaning this terrible tragedy?"

"Yeah, but —" said Leyton.

"No buts," groaned Al-Ian. "This isn't the time for buts."

"I know," said Leyton. "It's just —"

"No, it's not just!" complained 3-M. "It's terribly unjust! And wrong and unfair!"

Leyton turned to Brendan and shrugged as if to say, "Hey, I tried."

Brendan smiled back. He raised his hand and snapped his fingers.

The ground began to shake. Wade, 3-M, Al-Ian, and Daisy looked up with startled expressions. Dirt began to slide down the sides of the huge hole. At the bottom of the hole, it covered Fibby's and Barton's and Ulna's feet.

"You better climb out of there before you get buried!" Daisy yelled.

"No way!" shouted Fibby. "I know a trick when I see one! You're not getting this gold!"

The ground continued to shake and more dirt slid down to the bottom of the hole. By now it had risen as high as Fibby's knees.

"Gold schmold, I'm out of here!" Barton yelled, and started to climb out of the hole.

Ulna pulled at her daughter's hand. *"Come on, Fibby! Now that you've claimed the gold, it's yours. We can come back and get it after the earth stops shaking!"*

"No way!" Fibby shouted. "As soon as I let go of this pot of gold, they'll figure out a way to steal it from me!"

Barton climbed out of the hole. He stood next to Daisy and quoted Mignon McLaughlin,[40] "In the arithmetic of love, one plus one equals everything."

"Barton, why do you keep quoting love poetry to me?" Daisy asked.

"To show you how I feel," Barton answered. "And I drive a BladeX scooter and wear Yike sneakers and listen to a Green pPod to impress you with my cool stuff."

"Cool stuff doesn't impress me," said Daisy. "But your poetry does."

"Really?" Barton's eyes widened.

The ground kept shaking. By now the dirt was up to Fibby's waist, but she still

---

[40] An American writer who briefly pitched in the Scottish Ladies' Tea and Softball League in the 1930s.

wouldn't give up the pot of gold. Ulna let go of her daughter's hand and started to climb out of the hole.

"You better get out of there before you're buried alive!" Daisy yelled to Fibby.

But Fibby shook her head. "I don't care. I'd rather go down with the ship!"

"That's an idiom!" Leyton shouted.

"*Fibby, please!*" Ulna yelled as the loose dirt rose toward Fibby's shoulders. "*It's not worth being buried for!*"

Then the most amazing thing happened. An enormous finger, as thick as a baseball bat, poked up through the dirt. Then another poked through, and another, until a whole giant hand the size of a large chair reached up through the dirt and took hold of the pot.

"No!" Fibby cried, up to her neck in

dirt and still clinging to the pot. "This is my gold!"

A second giant hand clawed its way through the dirt at the bottom of the hole. It closed around Fibby and gently pulled her away from the pot of gold.

"Noooooo!!!!" Fibby wailed. "I want my gold!"

Huge forearms rose out of the ground. Everyone backed away as two enormous elbows[41] appeared. Fibby squirmed and tried to fight her way out of the humongous hand that held her, but it wouldn't let go.

And then, suddenly . . . an enormous head the size of a refrigerator poked out of the bottom of the hole!

---

[41] The creases of elbows this large might contain close to a billion bacteria.

"Ah!" Fibby screamed, and everyone stepped back even farther. Dirt fell from the giant's long, shaggy hair and slid down his forehead. He had a huge wart between his eyes, and thick black hairs grew from his nose. He shook his head and dirt flew in all directions. Then, resting his elbows on the edge of the hole, he pulled himself up until his shoulders popped out of the hole.

"Why do I think that's the sleeping giant?" asked Wade.

"Because he crawled out of the ground and looks really grumpy?" guessed Leyton.

Fibby kept screaming and fighting, but the giant wouldn't let her go. He glared at the Tardy Boys and their friends. Then he snarled, revealing ginormous, yellow, crooked, and broken teeth.

"It's my gold!" Fibby shouted, and

pounded her fists against the giant's hand. "Give it back!"

"Arrrrgghhh!" the giant growled, and tightened his grip on the pot of gold. Then he pulled himself entirely out of the hole and stood up.

"Look out!" Wade shouted.

Crash! When the giant stood, his head and shoulders smashed through the skylight. Shards of broken glass showered down around the Tardy Boys and their friends. The giant shook the broken glass out of his hair.

Brendan stepped forward, and the giant reached down. He let go of Fibby and picked up the little pointy-eared mythological being of Irish descent.

"Stop!" Fibby screamed. "You can't take my gold, you big giant thief!"

The giant ignored her. Sitting in the

giant's hand, Brendan waved good-bye to the Tardy Boys and their friends.

Then, holding the pot of gold in one hand and Brendan in the other, the giant climbed up through the broken skylight and thumped away from The School With No Name.

"Mother!" Fibby turned and shouted at Ulna. "Since the giant took that pot of gold you have to go out and buy me another one!"

Ulna Mandible rolled her eyes and shook her head. Tired of her daughter's demands, she walked out of the school lobby and back to the Hummer.

"Mother!" Fibby shrieked, and followed her. "Where are you going? I gave you an order!"

But Ulna ignored her and got into the Hummer. Fibby had just enough time to jump into the passenger seat before her mother drove away.

Meanwhile, Barton had a big smile on his face.

"What's so funny?" asked Al-Ian.

Barton opened his fist. Inside were five gold coins. "I've got just enough gold to pay back Hammerhead Charlie with interest."

But then, before everyone's eyes, all five gold coins turned to dust.

"Darn!" Barton grumbled.

"Looks like Hammerhead Charlie's going to put the bite on you," said Leyton.

Barton's eyes widened with terror. Then he turned and ran.

HUBBA
HUBBA
WUBBA
LUBBA ♥

The Tardy Boys and their friends walked home. Now that the rain had ended, the sun once again disappeared behind gray photochemical smog.

"Brendan looked really happy that he got his pot of gold back," said Al-Ian.

"He's lucky to have a sleeping giant as a friend," said Leyton.

"You mean a large, shaggy-headed,

mythological being of Irish descent," said Daisy.

"How do you know he's not a large, ugly-toothed, mythological being of Irish descent?" asked Leyton.

"Given a choice between being a large shaggy-headed being and a large ugly-toothed being, what would you want to be called?" Wade asked.

"Leyton," said Leyton.

"That wasn't one of the choices," said Wade.

"But that's what I'm called," said Leyton.

"But what if you were a giant?" asked 3-M.

"I'd fix my teeth, brush my hair, and get that wart removed," said Leyton.

"That's not what we're talking about," said Wade.

"It's what I'm   about," said
Leyton.
Thanks to the J   Omnitron,
you, the reader, ca
wished they were t   the others

1) Even though th
   Omnitron still c
   Al-Ian's Velostat
   Helmet, it is safe
   he wants to tell hi
   Wubba Lubba ♥ no
   another school.

2) 3-M is deciding that
   another school because
   to stay close to the cute, thou
   slightly strange, boy who wears
   foil-covered shoulder pads and a
   Velostat Thought-Screen Helmet.

...all players Alex
... Jeter that he is
...ave extra tickets to

great A...

great A...
Ro...

...ing three tickets so that
...Catherine Zeta-Jones and
...ansson to the same game
...can fight over him. The Arthur
...hat if he can get Catherine Zeta-
...and Scarlett Johansson to fight on
...onal TV, then he can sell tickets to
...e fight.

...Want to see Catherine Zeta-Jones and
Scarlett Johansson duke it out on national
TV? Just send one pot of gold and a
stamped, self-addressed envelope to:

> The Arthur
> Round Table Lane
> End of the Rainbow, Ireland